KILLINGS AT LETANA CREEK

Retired United States Marshal Ned Thomas rides to Letana Creek to help a friend who fears being the next victim of a serial killer. But Ned makes matters worse for his friend's family and puts his own life in danger. Ned will need all his guile to solve the mystery surrounding the killings and to confront the Molloy brothers, unexpectedly released from prison. They are hell-bent on revenge. But those who write him off as a has-been are sorely mistaken . . .

Books by Bill Williams
in the Linford Western Library:

ESCAPE FROM FORT ISAAC
KILLER BROTHERS

BILL WILLIAMS

KILLINGS AT LETANA CREEK

Complete and Unabridged

LINFORD
Leicester

First published in Great Britain in 2005 by
Robert Hale Limited
London

First Linford Edition
published 2006
by arrangement with
Robert Hale Limited
London

British Library CIP Data

Williams, Bill
  Killings at Letana Creek.—Large print ed.—
Linford western library
1. Western stories
2. Large type books
I. Title
823.9′2 [F]

ISBN 1–84617–359–0

Published by
F. A. Thorpe (Publishing)
Anstey, Leicestershire

Set by Words & Graphics Ltd.
Anstey, Leicestershire
Printed and bound in Great Britain by
T. J. International Ltd., Padstow, Cornwall

1

Retired United States Marshal Ned Thomas had been intending to visit his old army friend Josh Stone soon, but in better circumstances than those he faced now. He had read the telegram six times even though the message was simple, Josh Stone needed help. Two men had been murdered and Josh had good reason to believe that he would be next. Thomas hadn't seen Stone for close to ten years, but he was special, like family. He knew that they would pick up as though it were yesterday. Things were like that with genuine friends, especially one that had saved your life as Josh had done.

Ned Thomas was fifty-six years old, a good three inches taller than most men, and despite the bullet wounds that he'd suffered in the line of duty, was in good health. The steely grey hair and beard were still kept neatly trimmed even though he had been retired for nearly a year. Some thought that the black eye-patch that covered his missing eye made him look distinguished whilst others thought it made him look even more fearsome.

Thomas had been married to his second wife Olive for only three months, and she didn't take kindly to the news that he was going to Letana Creek at sun-up tomorrow. She had lost her first husband to consumption, just before Thomas's first wife, Mary had fallen to the same illness four years ago. It wasn't a match made in heaven, but they had been friends and Thomas persuaded her that they would be good company for each other.

'I'm too old for all that romancing stuff, but I'll look after you, Olive, and that's a promise,' he'd said by way of a proposal. Despite not being an offer that she couldn't refuse she had been happy with her marriage to Thomas and now their new life together was being endangered by a telegraph message from out of the blue.

Olive wouldn't ask him not to go because it would have been a waste of time, but she still feared that he was making a big mistake. She bit her tongue when she watched him after supper as he struggled to buckle on his gun belt before he gave up and skewered an extra hole in the belt to make allowances for his thickening waist. She marvelled at the speed at which he stripped down and cleaned his pistol, wondering how many men it had been used to kill. Ned was different from her Henry who had been a quiet, almost timid man, and the sort who would go out of his way to avoid trouble whilst Ned would confront it. She was thinking that Ned should be spending his days fishing, and evenings watching the sun go down from his chair on the porch. He'd earned a long retirement after fighting other people's battles, making the territory a better place to live in.

Olive had crept out of bed earlier than usual to prepare breakfast. When Thomas sat at the table a short time later he didn't have much of an appetite, but he made sure he left a clean plate. She would have sensed by the way he had tossed and turned in bed last night that he was worrying about making the trip. He wasn't a fool and he knew more than anyone that he wasn't the same man he'd been just a couple of years ago. He still had his strength, but he'd slowed down, mellowed in some ways. Some would say that he'd lost his edge. If he was going to help his friend he would have to rely upon his experience and guile more than anything else.

'You're a crafty one, Olive, serving up my special of eggs and beans with extra rashers of bacon thrown in. You're hoping I'll miss your cooking so much that I'll want to hurry back and then you'll give me those gardening jobs to finish off.'

She'd vowed to herself that she wouldn't say anything to dissuade him from going, but now she couldn't stop herself.

'Have you really got to go, Ned? Why can't the sheriff in Letana Creek help your friend?'

He sensed the fear that had prompted the question.

'Now listen, honey, I'm not going to be doing anything silly. There's a good chance that Josh's problem will have been sorted out by the time I get there. I'll have a few beers with him, catch up on old times and head back the following day. I'll be home before you know it.'

After he had given her a kiss and a hug that had lasted longer than usual, he stroked the smooth skin that belonged to a woman much younger than Olive's fifty-three years. He brushed aside the fair hair that had only the slightest trace of grey. Life hadn't been easy for Olive, having miscarried five times before she had been forced to accept that she would never have children. Then the loss of her beloved Henry had left her life in tatters. Ned was always protective towards her and had never uttered a cross word, but she had never loved him, not in the way she had Henry, at least not until now. She had sensed by his gentleness and the concern on his face that he didn't want to leave her. Olive also believed that he loved her as well, but she knew that she might have to wait a long time for him to declare it.

Thomas reached for the reins of the black stallion that had been presented to him by the US Army, unaware that Olive was fighting back the tears, not wishing to make things more difficult for him. He grunted as he swung his right leg over and positioned himself in the saddle. The stallion moved, perhaps objecting to the bulk on his back.

'Now you'd better behave yourself,' Thomas said. He smiled at Olive. 'Not you, honey, I mean this ornery feller. I think the jury's still out as to who's master in our partnership, perhaps by the time I've been to Letana Creek and back it will have been decided.'

2

The last two weeks had shown Cliff Myers that being deputy sheriff of Letana Creek was more trouble than he'd expected. It had seemed a quiet town and he hadn't figured the job was going to involve the trouble that had come his way recently. Myers was twenty-one years old, with the kind of good looks that most women liked and some men begrudged. The black curly hair was combed more times in a day than most men's received in a week or more and his expression oozed confidence. He was broad-shouldered and slim-hipped and made sure his clothes showed off his physique.

Myers had been adjusting his collar, and using the window as a mirror when he saw the men approaching the sheriff's office. He turned away and addressed Sheriff Brannigan who was seated at his desk.

'Here comes trouble, Sheriff. We've got a deputation from the town council.'

Dan Brannigan was not the sort to get ruffled. He remained seated as the six men crowded into the office. Brannigan was thirty-five years old, thickset, with the start of a beer belly. But Brannigan's blue eyes and slow, easy smile made him almost as popular with the ladies as Myers.

Jeff Lowrie, who ran the local store and was chairman of the council, was already red in the face before he started his verbal attack on the lawmen. Lowrie was best described as rotund in appearance; his specially imported glasses were usually rested towards the end of his pug nose. The dark brown eyes were cold and unblinking and his face had an expression that suggested that he was permanently agitated by something or other. Most folks regarded him as a bully of a man who had few friends except those he had bought. Lowrie had lived in Letana all his life and didn't like outsiders, except when they were parting with their money in his store. The store still provided him with a modest income but it had earned him a fortune during the height of the mining that had long since run out. Now Lowrie's ambition was to become governor of the state and he would get there even if he had to buy his way to the governor's house. In the meantime he would play local politics.

'You're not going to stop another killing while you're sat on your butt, Sheriff, and your useless deputy is gazing out of the window.'

Myers was about to respond to Lowrie's outburst when Brannigan raised his hand as a signal for him to hold off.

'If you come up with some evidence for us then we'll be glad to investigate,' Brannigan said calmly, displaying no sign that he felt threatened by his accusers.

'That's what you're paid for,' shouted

Henry Mason. There was a nervous tremor in his voice, and it lacked the aggression and conviction of Lowrie's. Mason was a slim, wiry man. The thin moustache looked as though it had been painted on, just like the dark wisps of hair that were held in place by some sort of lotion.

Brannigan smiled. 'I'm surprised that you're complaining, Mr Mason, seeing as how your undertaker's business is thriving. At the moment you're a prime suspect because you certainly have a motive. I'm told that it isn't cheap to get buried in this town.'

Mason was too shocked by the suggestion to make a response and Lowrie's face looked as though a blood-vessel was about to explode as he inched even closer to the desk.

'The murder of three good men inside of two weeks is no joking matter, Sheriff, and you'd better apologize to Henry Mason for your cheap remarks.'

Brannigan stood up and tucked his shirt into his pants. Those nearest the desk wondered what his next move would be, and it seemed an age before he spoke.

'You're right, Mr Lowrie, and I'm truly sorry for teasing Mr Mason, but despite what you might think, no one wants to catch the killer more than Cliff and me. I understand that feelings are running high and perhaps it's best if I hand in my badge while you good folks are here. Cliff and me discussed this earlier, and we were wondering if someone else should make a fresh start; perhaps a local man would have more success.'

Cliff Myers was thinking that Brannigan was a crafty devil because there had been no talk of resigning. Jeff Lowrie was remembering how difficult it was to hire lawmen, which was why they had finished up with two inexperienced men in the first place.

'Now let's not be hasty, Sheriff,' said Lowrie in a tone that lacked its previous aggression, and even became conciliatory. 'All we're saying is that the investigation isn't getting anywhere, but that doesn't mean we want you to leave. Isn't that so, gentlemen?' There was a mumbled chorus of agreement from the deputation.

Brannigan paused, clearly showing his reluctance to respond.

'Well, as long as you're sure about wanting us to carry on, then I promise that we'll do our best. As it happens we do have a possible suspect for the last killing. I don't want to say too much at this stage, but we might be making an arrest soon.'

There was a buzz of excitement amongst the council members and some wanted more information, but Brannigan explained that it was early days, still, he was hopeful. In the meantime they must be patient and vigilant in case the killer struck again.

By the time Jeff Lowrie led the way out of the office the mood of the council had been transformed. Several of the members thanked Brannigan and shook his hand.

Cliff Myers waited until the door was closed before he gave a short whistle, shook his head and then smiled.

'I've got to hand it to you, Sheriff. You managed that with such . . .' Myers struggled for the right word and settled on ' . . . poise'.

'They have reason to be unhappy, but Lowrie's all bluster. He's a typical politician, who likes to look important. The secret is to let them feel that they're in control. It works every time.'

The young deputy was looking worried when he questioned the sheriff about what he would do if they hadn't produced the mystery suspect within a couple of days.

'No worries on that score. If we don't get lucky in the next few days then we'll bring in Karl Tadcaster for the murder of Jack Beamish.'

Myers wondered what Brannigan was up to now, because it was the first time that Karl Tadcaster's name had been mentioned, and he wasn't someone who would have been on his list of suspects.

'They say that Tadcaster's one for the ladies, but he don't strike me as the sort who would end up killing those men.'

'The trouble with you, Myers, is that you don't have enough imagination. It's common knowledge that Tadcaster tried to bed the wife of every man who he's worked for. I've found out that he's done odd jobs around the places of all the dead men and had arguments with them about their womenfolk. He was working at the Beamish place just two days before Jack Beamish ended up laid out in Henry Mason's funeral parlour with a bullet in his back, just like the others.'

'But Beamish's wife Doreen is old enough to be Tadcaster's ma, and they ain't got any daughters he could have gone lusting after.'

'According to the talk in Garrety's saloon it seems that Tadcaster isn't put off by age or looks. If it's female then that's all that matters. Fat, ugly or old don't matter none to him, just so long as it wears a dress. By the way, how are you getting on with young Shelley Stone?'

Myers told him that he was still seeing her, but Josh Stone had been making sure that there was always a chaperon around and they couldn't do anything but talk. He didn't tell the sheriff that he had the impression that Josh Stone wasn't keen on him seeing Shelley, and would probably try and split them up if he could.

3

The sun had only been up for an hour when Josh Stone heeled his black mare out of the small stable at the back of his ranch house. Perhaps a good day working out in the open mending some fences would give him time to think. He'd been feeling the same kind of nervousness in recent days that he'd experienced during the war when he was dreading the moment a sniper's bullet would thud into his body. He hadn't slept properly for more than a week and that didn't help his nerves any. Stone hadn't wanted to alarm his wife, Barbara about the danger that he felt he was in and had merely mentioned that his old friend, Ned Thomas might make a visit soon. Stone still hoped that his fears might all be down to his imagination, but he didn't think so.

Josh Stone was fifty-two years old and apart from a bad back caused by years of bending and lifting more than he should, he was in fine health. He'd lost most of his hair in recent years and had to put up with some teasing from his son Ralph. The face had more than a fair share of worry lines even though until recently he hadn't had much to worry about, apart from his daughter seeing Deputy Myers. Myers was pleasant enough and popular, but there was something about him that he didn't trust.

Stone had checked at the telegraph office every day since he'd wired Thomas nearly a week ago, but so far there had been no reply. He would try again today in case his friend might have been away until now. Stone had told Barbara to look out for Thomas, explaining that he would likely be wearing an eye-patch because he'd lost an eye some years ago when a broken bottle had been thrust in to his face. He could always send another wire, but there didn't seem any point when there was a good chance that Thomas might even be dead.

By late morning he'd managed to make good progress with the fence-mending. He took a short break to eat the bread and cheese that Barbara had packed for him and then washed it down with the bottle of warm beer. He was ready to restart work when he saw the rider approaching. He couldn't think what would bring him out here, unless Josh's worst fear was about to be realized. So many things flashed through his mind. He wished that he hadn't been so irritable with Barbara last night or given Shelley another lecture about Myers. He should have confided in someone other than Thomas, but he had been fearful that they might have thought he was being foolish. Well, it was too late for regrets. He had either to make the first move and challenge his suspect or bide his time, and that might cost him his life. Stone had kept his weapon strapped on even though it had been uncomfortable while he was working. He moved his hand to cover the butt of the pistol, then felt a massive sense of relief when the suspect waved to him as he passed by, apparently in a hurry and heading towards town.

The incident left Stone feeling stupid and he scolded himself for simply not confronting the man. He resolved to lighten up and have a different approach to things. He would slacken the reins on his children, and that would mean giving Myers a chance to prove himself. After all, Myers was a lawman and that must be something in his favour. He would also stop trying to push Ralph; he would let him develop at his own pace. He loved the boy and would start enjoying his time with him.

Stone felt good, better than he had for some time. He had put everything into perspective. He would start behaving normally again and that meant unbuckling his gun belt and hanging it on the fence, enabling him to move more easily as he bent down to unroll the barbed wire. The worried look had left his face and he was no longer edgy or on his guard, which was why he hadn't seen that the rider was heading back in his direction.

4

By the time Thomas pulled up the stallion at the signpost that told him that Letana Creek was just two miles away, he was wishing that Josh's message had arrived a day earlier so that he could have caught the weekly train out of Statton Crossing. The train would have taken him within thirty miles of Letana Creek and saved him an almost two-day trek across the Arizona desert. The stallion had behaved himself and he had been wise to refuse to take the mountain pass route yesterday, otherwise they both might have ended up as a meal for the vultures at the foot of some mountain.

According to the rough map that Stone had sent him some years ago, he lived on this side of town, but off towards the west. Thomas could never be accused of being vain, but he didn't want to give Stone's wife the impression that he was some kind of saddle-bum, which was how he felt at the moment after the effects of the journey. He was tempted to go to town first and tidy himself up, but then figured that the Stones would make allowances for his appearance, so he heeled his mount in the direction of the narrow trail that wound its way to the west. Maybe it would have been better to have sent Stone a reply to his message, but it was too late to worry about that now. The sun was hotter than it had been since he left Statton Crossing three days ago, and his shirt was stuck to his skin. His mouth had the sort of dryness that could only be fully relieved by a cool beer. He hoped Josh had good supply.

* * *

The sign that read STONE'S RANCH was in need of a lick of paint, but the house ahead looked in good shape, at least from a distance. It was nothing special, but a good family house, and no doubt a happy one. The black-and-white mongrel was taking his guard duties too seriously for Thomas's liking and he feared that the stallion would launch the family pet into the air if it ventured any closer. The yapping stopped when the skinny young feller came out of the barn that was close to the house. He was carrying a rifle which was pointing towards the ground, but the scowl on his face signalled a welcome no better than the dog had given.

'What brings you this way, mister?' the young feller asked as he squinted into the sun behind Thomas. 'There's no work here if that's what you're looking for.'

'I'm looking for Josh Stone,' replied Thomas.

'There's no one here except me, and Pa didn't say he was expecting anyone to come calling.' Thomas could see that the boy was suspicious. He must have been about eighteen and was nothing like his pa had looked as a young man. He was fair-haired and on the delicate side, perhaps favouring his ma.

'I'm a friend of your pa's. My name's Ned Thomas. I expect your pa has mentioned me?'

Ralph Stone frowned.

'No, I've never heard him talk about you, but if you want to see Pa, he's mending some fences in one of our fields about half a mile from here. He plans to go into town when he's finished.'

'What's your name, boy?'

'Ralph,' he answered after a pause, lowering his eyes.

Thomas left the Stones' ranch regretting he hadn't remembered the boy's name from one of Stone's letters. It might have made the kid less jumpy if he'd revealed that he knew his name, but at least he'd told him where to find his pa.

Half an hour later he was thinking that he hadn't listened to the directions properly or young Ralph had deliberately misled him. Thomas hoped the boy had at least been telling the truth about Josh's plans to ride into town later because that was where Thomas would head. But first he would take a short rest by the river he'd just spotted. He would stay here awhile in the hope that Stone might just come by because, according to the signpost, the trail beside the river led to town.

Thomas made himself comfortable in the long, soft grass near the riverbank. He felt strange, knowing that his friend might just be a couple of fields away. The last time that they'd met was when Stone had been on a cattle drive which had passed near Statton Crossing. They'd promised to keep in touch, but had let things drift, as friends often do. Then when Thomas's wife had died it didn't seem right somehow, but he had thought of Stone from time to time when he'd told the tale about the man who had saved his life. The war had been over for a week and they had been heading back to camp when they strayed into some Indian territory. As well as Stone, there were five others in their group. One of them was Jonjo Beale, who reckoned that he knew enough of the Indian language to communicate with them.

Beale soon got his chance to show off his linguistic talent when a party of ten braves blocked their path and started making menacing noises. Jonjo had stepped forward and started doing lots of jabbering and hand-waving. Thomas remembered how impressed he had been when the braves quietened down and started smiling. When the braves turned their ponies around and rode off some of the men gave Jonjo the thumbs up and slapped him on the back. The congratulations bestowed on him were cut short when the air was filled with an Indian battle cry as the braves turned and charged them. Jonjo was the first to die from the arrow that entered his left eye and pierced his brain. The braves had the advantage of surprise and numbers, but Thomas and the troop that he was in charge of were battle-hardened and they had fire-power. Before the soldiers had suffered a second casualty more than half their attackers had been gunned down, but it didn't stop the rest from fighting on. Thomas's gun had jammed and as he had reached out to pick up a weapon dropped by one of his fallen comrades, the leader of the braves dismounted from his pony and slashed him across the right cheek. The dark curly hair that Thomas had possessed as a younger man had been grabbed by the brave who was ready to scalp him when Stone had fired the shot that saved Thomas's life. When the fighting ended, leaving the braves dead or dying, only Thomas, Stone and a man named Jerome had survived the attack. Jerome told Thomas that Stone had saved him with his last bullet, and then had to kill another Indian with a knife because he had run out of ammunition. The trio were lucky to be alive, but Jerome had received an enormous gash to his leg which meant that they couldn't continue their journey. After they'd buried their dead, Thomas and Stone had carried Jerome away from the 'battlefield' and made camp. The following day, Jerome's wound was badly infected and he urged Thomas and Stone to continue the journey back to their camp and fetch some help.

It was over a week later when Stone was able to return to the spot where they had left Jerome, but he wasn't there and he was never found. The memory of Jerome dying on his own, being carried off by a bear or dragged away by wolves had haunted Thomas for years and he suspected that Stone must have felt the same.

★ ★ ★

Thomas awoke from his snooze, pulled the gold watch from his waistcoat and discovered that he'd been at the spot near the river for almost two hours. After splashing his face in the cold water of the river he mounted the stallion and heeled it in the direction of town, hoping to meet Stone.

As Thomas looked down Main Street he doubted if there was a prettier town than Letana Creek in the whole of the state. Many of the buildings looked as if they had been erected as permanent structures, unlike many of those in the mining towns. The array of flowers along the boardwalks gave the place a homely feel, and he was thinking that Olive would like it here.

The sign at the entrance to town had listed the population, but Thomas guessed that it wasn't accurate in view of recent happenings. The next sign he saw was outside the barber's shop, which was tempting and it made him smile. It read: WASH AWAY THAT DUST WITH A BATH AT CHARLIE'S. The little fat man who gave him a cheery smile must have been Charlie. Although the town had a nice orderly feel about it, he still intended to leave the stallion at the livery while he had a stroll around town and made a visit to the saloon. There were several horses tied to the various hitch rails, but the stallion might just prove too tempting for some son of a bitch horse-thief. By the time he reached half-way down Main Street he could see what looked like the livery towards the far end of the street, but he slowed his horse down when he saw the large crowd gathered outside the sheriff's office.

Thomas was surprised by the hostility of the men who were all looking in his direction, but not as much as he was by the sight of young Ralph Stone who was still holding his rifle.

'That's him!' Ralph shouted, 'That's the one-eyed man who killed my pa.' Ralph's voice was tearful, as well as angry. As Ralph raised his rifle to the firing position, Thomas's right hand gripped his own pistol, but against all his natural instinct he paused, and the weapon was still holstered when the bullet thudded into his left shoulder. Thomas fell from his horse but he still heard someone in the crowd shout, 'Let's hang the bastard.'

Thomas was dazed by the fall, oblivious to the ructions that followed and unaware that Barbara Stone had rushed from the boardwalk and was gazing down at him. She had been consoling her daughter, Shelley, outside the store after Ralph had told her about Josh being killed. She had seen the rider with the black eye-patch just a second before Ralph had fired the shot, but had been too late to shout to her son.

'He's the one who came looking for Pa,' Ralph explained to Barbara Stone after he and the rest of the crowd had crossed the street and stood hovering over Thomas.

'You've made a terrible mistake, Ralph,' Barbara Stone cried out, filled with her own guilt for forgetting to tell Ralph that his pa was expecting an old friend to come calling and that he would be wearing an eye-patch. The pale face of Ralph turned ashen when his ma told him that he had probably just shot his pa's friend who was a United States marshal. Ralph had told Sheriff Brannigan that he had been suspicious of the man who had called at their ranch, and had decided to go and check if his pa was all right. He had found him lying face down. Josh Stone had been shot in the back, and he was dead.

Brannigan tried to restore some calm and ordered his deputy to go and get Doc Shultz and then addressed the crowd.

'You heard Mrs Stone. This man's a US marshal. Now you'd best go about your business.'

'If he's a marshal, then where's his badge?' shouted one of the mob.

'That's right! Where's his badge?' shouted another.

Brannigan knelt down beside Thomas who was lying on his back, and pulled out the marshal's badge from Thomas's waistcoat pocket. There were gasps from the crowd and an anguished cry of: 'What have I done, Ma?' from Ralph Stone.

'Someone go and find out what's happened to Doc Shultz,' ordered Brannigan with an urgency that hadn't been there when he had sent Myers to get the doctor. Brannigan removed his neckerchief and was pressing it against the wound in Thomas's shoulder when a breathless Doc Shultz arrived and removed the blood-sodden cloth from the wound. The doc was calm as he asked for some men to carry his patient to the tiny surgery which was across the street, next to Lowrie's store. As Thomas was carried away, Brannigan told Ralph Stone that he was under arrest, in a tone that was softer than it might have been had the boy's ma not been there.

Sheriff Brannigan had planned to arrest Karl Tadcaster later, but now he would have to try and link Tadcaster to the death of Josh Stone. Once Ralph Stone was secured in one of the cells, Brannigan and Myers discussed the events that had produced another killing, and perhaps the death of a US marshal.

'It seems a bit odd that Ralph knew nothing about his pa's friend,' Brannigan mused.

'Not really,' replied Myers. 'They're not what you might call a talkative family and Ralph's a bit weird, but we get on well. To be honest I didn't think he had it in him to plug the marshal like that, nor the inclination, because Ralph and his pa were not exactly close. In fact I think Ralph hated him.'

Brannigan leaned back in his seat and stretched his arms towards the ceiling.

'I don't suppose you'll be too upset now that Josh is out of the way, especially if Ralph isn't around either.'

Myers was taken back by the directness of Brannigan's remark, but he could hardly deny that things had been strained between him and Shelley's pa, especially after Josh had made it clear that he didn't approve of him seeing Shelley.

'It's true that I won't miss Josh, but I didn't want to see him dead, if that's what you mean. I tried my best with him, but for some reason he just had a down on me. I thought things might have got better when I told him that my pa served in the army at the same time as him, but it didn't.'

'Shelley's a lovely-looking woman. The sort that some men would kill for,' said Brannigan. When Myers didn't respond to his jibe he turned his thoughts to Marshal Thomas.

'I'd like to know what brought the marshal to our little paradise,' Brannigan mused. 'I've had lots of chinwags with Josh Stone, but he never mentioned being friendly with a United States marshal.'

'I wonder how the old feller's getting on over at the surgery, or the 'meat house', as some folks call it,' Myers pondered. 'He was in pretty bad shape when I left him and the doc's record at saving his patients isn't too good. Is it true that Doc Shultz was a butcher back home in some place called Germany?'

'So they say,' replied Brannigan, 'and according to some, he hasn't changed his trade. I'm not sure about the doc coming from Germany though. His English seems too good and I've noticed that he lets his accent slip. Sometimes he says whiskey and other times its vhiskey.'

'What, you mean he's some kind of an impostor?' Myers asked.

'I've no idea,' Brannigan replied. 'I think I'd better go over and see how the marshal's doing. He seems a bit long in the tooth to be a lawman, but he looks as though he could handle himself. You stay here and make sure no one starts anything. You best get one of those rifles out of the cabinet and keep it handy. Pointing a rifle at a crowd always makes them wary about trying anything.'

'Sure thing, Sheriff, but what are you

going to do about arresting Karl Tadcaster?'

'Let me worry about that,' Brannigan snapped back, before he reached for his hat and then stepped out on to Main Street.

5

Thomas came to, thinking that he was still in the nightmare that he'd been having. The face of the man grinning down at him wasn't a pretty sight. The man's lips were dry, and very pale, making his yellowish teeth all the more noticeable. Both his eyes were almost closed but open wide enough to reveal that the parts that should have been white were red.

'Welcome back, Marshal. I thought you were a goner for a while,' Doc Shultz said, then added:

'It's only a small wound, but you bled like a pig. I expect you'd like a drink. It should be water, but a drop of whiskey will ease your pain.'

Thomas let his gaze drift around the tiny room that contained an array of surgical instruments, and a lot of what he assumed was his blood.

'Is Josh Stone dead?' Thomas asked when the old geezer returned with his drink, spilling some of it, unable to control his shaking hand.

'I'm afraid so and that makes number four. I believe you were a friend.'

'I am — I was,' replied Thomas correcting himself. 'Where's the doc who patched me up?'

'The town doesn't have a doctor, but most people call me Doc Shultz.'

Thomas tried to sit up, shocked at the news that the grimy little fellow with the dirty fingernails might have been poking around with some of the rusty implements that lay on the table.

Thomas offered his thanks to Shultz, but he was already wondering if they were warranted. Only time would tell if his helper had done him more harm than good. He declined a second whiskey, but it didn't stop Shultz from helping himself to another full glass of his favourite drink.

'What's happened to Josh's boy?' Thomas asked.

'Don't worry; Sheriff Brannigan has thrown him in jail. He's a nice kid, but I expect he'll face a hanging for trying to kill you. You being a United States Marshal will make that a certainty.'

Thomas was feeling guilty enough that he had arrived too late to help his friend; now, to make matters worse he might end up becoming unwittingly responsible for the death of Josh Stone's son.

'I'm actually a retired marshal, but how did you find out that I was lawman?'

'Barbara Stone said you were. If she hadn't, then I guess you'd have ended up dangling from some tree and young Ralph would be a hero now. It was just as well that you were carrying that badge.'

Thomas hadn't heard most of what Shultz had said because he had lost consciousness.

As Brannigan stepped on to the porch outside the doc's surgery he was approached by a small group of troublemakers.

'Is it true, that the marshal's dead and Ralph Stone's going to hang?' one of them asked. Brannigan ordered them to disperse and to forget any idea of stoking up trouble unless they wanted to join Ralph in the cells. They skulked away, sensing that the sheriff meant what he'd just threatened.

The smell that hit Brannigan upon entering the surgery reminded him of his visits to the saloon which was just a short distance away. The doc was slumped in a chair, but he sat upright as he awakened from his snooze. It looked as though the old marshal was alive, but he was whiter than a clean sheet on wash-day. The eye-patch had been removed and the gruesome hollow looked stark against the paleness of the skin. The remaining eye flickered open for a short while and Brannigan would be surprised if Thomas lasted the night.

'How's he doing, Doc? He doesn't look too good from here!'

'He's doing just fine. That rifle bullet took a bit of ferreting for because it had gone in so deep, but I got the svinehunt out. I tell you that feller there is as tough as they come. There wasn't a whimper from him all the time I was digging for that piece of lead, but judging by the scars on his body he isn't a stranger to pain.'

'So what are his chances? Folks are thinking that young Ralph will hang if he dies.'

'There's almost as much of his blood on the floor and in Main Street as there is in his body, but I can tell that this man's a survivor. If I can keep getting some liquids into him and I don't mean booze, then I think he'll pull through.'

Brannigan wasn't convinced, especially with the doc's record, and he doubted if he would get the chance to ask the marshal what had brought him to Letana Creek.

★ ★ ★

Brannigan returned to the surgery the following day and was surprised to see that Thomas was dressed in a fresh shirt and was tucking into a large helping of beans and eggs. The paleness had gone from his cheeks and he didn't look so terrifying now that he was wearing his eye-patch to hide the hole. After the doc had made the introductions, Brannigan expressed his surprise at the dramatic recovery.

'To be honest, Marshal, I thought you were destined for the cemetery last night, even though the doc was confident enough.'

Thomas smiled. 'My old ma used to say that only the good die young. By the way, you ought to know that I'm retired from the service. I carry the old badge as a good-luck charm. I'm just plain old Ned Thomas. I expect you might have thought that I was here on some kind of official business, but I would like to help find the yella-belly who killed my friend Josh Stone and perhaps those others. That's if you don't have any objections. It'll take me a day or two to regain my strength.'

Brannigan was taken aback by the request. The man he hadn't expected to survive the night was now offering to solve the mystery deaths. He didn't much like the idea of an outsider interfering, but felt that he could hardly refuse the offer of help. At least it might get the town council off his back.

'As long as you think you're up to it, Marshal. I didn't know Josh very well, but I liked him. I do have a handle on at least one of the killings and I'm planning to bring the man in soon, so it might all be over by the time you're ready to help. Incidentally, in case you have been worrying about that fine animal of yours, I've had him stabled at the livery. I can arrange for you to stay at the hotel if you like, unless you have some other plans.'

Thomas accepted his offer and told Brannigan that he would like to visit Ralph Stone later. He also enquired how the rest of Josh's family were coping because he had plans to see them as well. He wanted to offer his condolences and thank Barbara Stone for saving his life.

6

It was just before noon when Thomas took a very slow walk across Main Street to the sheriff's office. By the time he had climbed the three steps on to the porch he was feeling weak and almost faint which served as a reminder that healing took longer than it used to. He didn't intend to be silly, but neither did he intend a single slug to put him out of action for long.

Thomas prided himself on being a good judge of character and within seconds of being introduced to Cliff Myers he had decided that there was something about him that he didn't like. He didn't feel any better about things when Brannigan told him that the young deputy was courting Josh's daughter, Shelley.

The meeting with young Ralph was never going to be easy, and when

Thomas was let into Ralph Stone's cell his mixture of emotions seemed bizarre.

Thomas wanted to tell Ralph what a good man, and a fine soldier his pa had been, but that could come later. First, he needed to know if the boy had seen any clues when he'd found his pa's body. He made him recount every last detail while it was fresh in his mind, no matter how insignificant it might appear. According to Ralph, only the family and Thomas himself would have known where his pa was at the time he was killed. That was, except Cliff Myers. The deputy had been at the house when Josh had mentioned his plans.

'What's going to happen to me, Marshal Thomas?' Ralph asked as Thomas prepared to leave the cell.

'I can't really say, son. I won't be pressing any charges for what you did, but it'll be up to Sheriff Brannigan what happens next.'

Ralph remained silent as he shook the outstretched hand of the man who had shown him such understanding and sympathy. Ralph looked a pathetic figure as he watched Thomas leave.

Brannigan was flicking through some wanted posters when Thomas came back into the main office.

'I don't expect that was too easy,' he remarked putting the posters back on the desk.

'The boy must be going through hell,' said Thomas and then asked Brannigan what he planned to do with Ralph.

'I was going to send for the judge later today, and then it's out of my hands,' Brannigan replied, sounding as if the whole thing was just a routine event.

'I'd like you to do me a big favour, Sheriff, and let the boy go. I won't be making any charges and I won't testify against him either.'

Brannigan wasn't surprised by the request, but the marshal might be about to change his mind.

'There's something you ought to

know about that boy in there, Marshal. I was talking to Myers about him last night and he reckons that the kid hated his pa. Josh was forever correcting him, like pas do. Trying to mould him I guess, but the kid felt that he couldn't do anything right. Myers was at the Stones' place the night before Josh died and witnessed an almighty row between Josh and Ralph. According to Myers the last thing that Ralph said to his pa before he stormed out was that he wished his pa was dead.'

'He's going through that mixed-up period between boyhood and manhood,' Thomas suggested. 'He wouldn't have realized that his pa was pushing him for his own good. He would have seen that in time, but just because he blurted something out when he was feeling under pressure doesn't mean that he meant it. Surely you're not suggesting that he shot his own pa and then tried to put the blame on me.'

'To be honest, Marshal, I just don't know what to think,' Brannigan sighed.

'It might be like you say and he was just a bit mixed up, but some kids are born crafty, and they'll pass the blame if they can.'

Thomas was beginning to get angry at the way this was developing. He would bet his last dollar that the boy was innocent.

'Hang on, Brannigan; we're not talking about a young boy being accused of stealing his sister's candy. I doubt if you've come across a fraction of the murderers that I have, and I'm telling you for free, that boy's innocent.'

Brannigan wasn't about to let Thomas pull rank on him. The boy was his prisoner and he would decide what to do with him, but he didn't want to rile Thomas more than he had to.

'Maybe he is innocent, but the fact is the kid took the law into his own hands when he took a pot-shot at you. He wanted you dead and that's a fact. But I've listened to what you've said and I plan to let him stew in jail for a couple of days. He'll be able to go to his pa's funeral of course. If he gets through that without cracking up and confessing to killing his pa, and nothing else turns up that implicates him, then I'll let him go.'

The tension left Thomas. 'That sounds fair to me, but I would like to tell his ma about your plans,' Thomas replied. 'I'll ask her to keep it to herself so that he's taught a lesson, which I suspect is your aim.'

Brannigan shrugged his shoulders.

'No problem. The poor woman's got enough trouble without fearing that her son might face a hanging.'

'I appreciate your help, Brannigan. Now I think I'll go and check on my horse and move into a room at the hotel.'

'It's all taken care of. They'll be expecting you,' Brannigan confirmed.

'Thanks, but there is one other thing you could help me with and that's draw up a list of the men who have been killed, including details of their age, what they did, how long they've lived here. It would also help if you added any thoughts of your own that you might have about possible suspects.'

Brannigan hid his displeasure when he replied:

'Sure, if you think it will help, but as I've already mentioned I plan to make an arrest very soon, so let's see how that goes first.'

When Thomas left the office, Brannigan was thinking that perhaps it might have been better to have declined Thomas's offer to help. He had a sneaking feeling that Thomas would soon be trying to take charge of the investigation and start doing things his way.

7

All of the folks that gathered at the cemetery for Josh's funeral were making their fourth appearance there in recent weeks, except for Thomas. He'd had a brief meeting with Barbara and Shelley before the funeral procession had left for the cemetery and expressed his sorrow at losing his old friend. He had been pleased to see the relief on Barbara Stone's face when he had mentioned the sheriff's intention to release Ralph in a few days. She displayed a sense of warmth despite the sadness she was obviously feeling. It seemed that Josh had chosen a plain but dependable woman, just as Thomas would have expected him to. In contrast, Shelley Stone was what most men would describe as a 'stunner'. She was tall and with a body to match the most curvy saloon girl. The blonde hair hung about her shoulders and the pale-blue eyes were striking, even though at present they were puffy through all the recent crying.

Ralph Stone's face was drawn and pale as he stood beside the two women. The widows and families of the other victims were nearby, having to relive their own tragic experiences. Thomas stayed a discreet distance away, not wishing to intrude in what was a family affair, but Myers was positioned behind Shelley Stone and near enough to keep an eye on Ralph. Thomas was surprised that Brannigan wasn't present and he wondered what the 'important business' was that had prevented his attendance.

The family held themselves together until the final moment when the coffin was lowered into the dark grave.

'Daddy, please don't leave us,' shrieked Shelley, followed by: 'Daddy, Daddy I always loved you.' She would have thrown herself on top of the coffin if Myers hadn't grabbed her.

At the end of the funeral service the

mourners made their way to the small hall beside the white wood-built church for the traditional gathering. Thomas still felt as though he was intruding, but the people of Letana Creek were good folks and some of them had approached him and enquired about his recovery. One of them was Lisa Norris, whose kindly face bore no signs of her recent loss and she had made a point of seeking him out.

'God moves in some strange ways at times,' she replied when Thomas had expressed his sympathy. 'My Len was no stranger to killing, Marshal. Len fought in the war, but he never spoke about it except just the once when he expressed his sorrow at having to take another life. I remember the day he left and the day he returned with Josh Stone. Of course they looked thinner, but it was their eyes that had changed most. There was a look of sadness and a deadness about them, but the men got over it, and now they are at peace.'

Thomas had known lots of folks who

had gained strength from their faith in times of tragedy, but none had been as strong as Lisa Norris.

'What about Luke Cutler and Jack Beamish. Were they former soldiers as well?' Thomas asked, lowering his voice in case any relatives were close enough to hear his question.

'Jack was, but Luke was only a young man, and half the age of the others who have been killed,' Lisa replied.

Thomas decided it was time to leave. He bade Lisa Norris farewell before making his way over to Barbara and Shelley Stone, who were standing alone now that Ralph had been taken back to the cells.

When Thomas said he would like to visit her in a few days, Barbara gave a weak smile and the pale-blue eyes brightened just a little, but he doubted if she had slept a wink during recent nights.

'I'd like that,' she replied. 'He told me that you might be coming, but he seemed a bit vague when I asked how long you would be staying. I was puzzled how he knew about your plans to visit because we hadn't received any mail for some weeks.' When she asked if his arrival was anything to do with the other killings he told her that he would explain everything when he visited her at home. He made an excuse to leave by claiming that he was feeling tired and was going back to the hotel to rest.

Thomas had reached the hotel entrance when he saw Brannigan hitch his horse to the rail outside his office. He was alone and obviously hadn't made the arrest that he'd mentioned.

Although Thomas had used his tiredness as an excuse for leaving the hall, he really was feeling weary by the time he reached his hotel room. He had barely loosened the starched collar when there was a hammering on the door, followed by some frantic shouting.

'Marshal, Marshal! Brannigan wants you over at the jailhouse. He said to tell you that it's important — I mean urgent, that's what he said.'

Thomas didn't know who the excited messenger was, but he called back:

'I'm on my way.'

He decided against changing out of his black suit and into more comfortable clothes. The tailor in town had fitted him out with the suit and he hoped to trade it in before he left. He had a perfectly good suit back home and with old Uncle Jimbo being his only surviving relative, he didn't plan on going to many more funerals before his own.

Brannigan was at the door of his office and looked grim-faced, which prompted Thomas to ask him if there'd been another killing.

Brannigan shook his head and then nodded in the direction of the open cell. Thomas was thinking that Ralph had just complicated things for himself by escaping.

'The young fool,' he growled, and then he saw the blood on the floor. Ralph Stone was dead, lying in his own blood, and it looked as though he had slashed his wrists.

'Goddam it,' Thomas groaned. He was already thinking of the fresh sorrow that would soon hit the Stone women-folk.

Brannigan was also thinking about the impact on the Stones, but from a personal point when he asked Thomas:

'I don't suppose you fancy breaking the news to the family, Marshal, you being a family friend an' all?'

Thomas could have pointed out to Brannigan that he hardly knew either of the women, but he didn't, and agreed to tell Barbara and Shelley.

Thomas couldn't get too close to the sad figure of Ralph without stepping in the blood, but he was able to get near enough to see the word SORRY scrawled in blood on the cream-coloured blanket that lay across the bed. The small knife that had been used to end a young life must have been thrown to the far end of the cell where the pool of red liquid had not quite reached. The sight of the knife made Thomas's own blood boil and Brannigan was taken by surprise when Thomas grabbed him by the throat and roared at him.

'How did the boy get hold of that knife when he was supposed to be in custody? This is your fault, Brannigan. The buck stops with you.' Thomas released his grip and pushed the choking Brannigan against the bars of the cell.

'Now hold on, Marshal. He didn't have a knife when I left here, and that's how I found him. He must have got it from someone at the funeral.'

'Jesus, what's happened here,' blurted out Myers, who had entered the office unnoticed.

'We were just wondering how the poor beggar managed to get hold of a knife,' said Brannigan.

Myers looked sheepish.

'I gave it to him when I brought him back after the funeral. He said that he wanted to do some whittling. I didn't see any harm seeing as how you planned to release him soon. I thought it would take his mind off his pa's funeral and all the upset.'

Now it was Brannigan's turn to be angry as he hurled abuse at his deputy.

'Did you tell him that he was being released soon?'

'No, I thought he already knew,' replied Myers.

'You damned fool!' Brannigan roared. 'The poor kid thought that he was still facing a hanging.'

Thomas had calmed down, and had some sympathy for Myers. At least he'd come clean about the knife and not tried to lie about it.

'Leave it be, Brannigan. All this hollering isn't going to bring him back and it isn't fair to blame Myers. It was just a tragic mistake. Perhaps we shouldn't have played games with the boy. Maybe we should have told him straight away that he wasn't going to be charged. So I guess we're all to blame in our own way.'

Brannigan sighed.

'You're right, Marshal, I'm sorry, Myers, I shouldn't have heaped the blame on you like I did.'

'We need to let his folks know before word gets out,' Thomas said, then addressed Brannigan. 'You'd better get the boy cleaned up and taken to the undertaker's. I'll take Myers with me so he can help break the news to the Stone womenfolk and then we'll take them to see the boy. You'd better make sure the undertaker works fast.'

Brannigan agreed with the plan of action, but he was none too keen about Thomas doing the ordering. The sooner Thomas recovered and left town, the better Brannigan would like it.

When Thomas reached the door he turned to face Brannigan.

'Perhaps it would be best if we kept Ralph's farewell message on the blanket a secret. It might be too upsetting for his ma. What do you think, Brannigan? It's your show and you must do what you think is best.'

Brannigan was pleased that at last his authority had been recognized.

'It seems sensible. I was going to suggest the same thing,' he lied.

Barbara Stone was surprised to see that Thomas had returned to the hall. Most of the people had offered their condolences once more and left, except for some of her very close friends. She had watched Thomas and Myers cross the room heading towards the minister. Whatever Thomas had said to the Reverend Booth she was certain that it involved her because they looked in her direction. When the three men walked towards her she sensed that something had happened and that it involved her dear Ralph. By the time that the trio reached her, and Thomas had started to say: 'I'm sorry, Ralph's dead,' she had silently repeated over and over: 'Please God, not Ralph as well.'

When she realized that her prayers had not been answered, Barbara Stone gave a short cry of despair. She thought that she had cried herself dry during the last few days, but it was not so. While Myers held on to the hysterical Shelley, her mother shook her head and simply asked:

'Why, dear God, why?'

Barbara's Stone's faith was strong and when she was taken to Mason's funeral parlour just a short while after hearing the tragic news she was no longer questioning God. She was thinking that there must be a good reason why Ralph had been taken from her. She would need to be extra strong for Shelley who had not been able to face seeing her dead brother and had stayed with Myers. Thomas was relieved to see that Ralph looked at peace, stretched out on the table surrounded by flowers. He had been dressed in a gown with long sleeves that hid the wounds to his wrists. Thomas placed a reassuring arm around her as she gazed at her son, and tenderly stroked Ralph's face.

Thomas took his arm away as she leaned forward and kissed her son's forehead.

'Such a sweet boy,' she said calmly, perhaps reassured that he was at peace. 'He loved his father despite their rows and now they are together in Heaven, of that I am certain.'

'Josh must have been very proud of him?' said Thomas, struggling to find the words that might give her some comfort.

She continued stroking her son's face, and smiled as she replied:

'He was, and he was so patient with Ralph, trying to teach him to read and write. Ralph was very sickly as a boy and missed a lot of schooling, and there's no denying that God had not blessed him with the brains of his sister. Try as he did, Josh couldn't teach him reading and writing. Now the boy will go to his grave without ever being able to write even his own name.'

'I'm sure that he had gifts that others didn't have,' Thomas consoled.

When Barbara Stone asked to be left alone with her son for a private moment, Thomas made his way outside to wait for her. He was still thinking about the scrawled '*Sorry*' message on the blanket in the cell. Either Ralph had learned to write without his ma knowing or someone else had done the writing on the blanket after murdering Ralph to make it look like suicide. Thomas intended to escort Barbara Stone back to the church hall where her daughter was and then he would ask Doc Shultz to examine the wounds on Ralph's wrists. Thomas would be interested in the doc's opinion as to whether Ralph's wounds had been self-inflicted.

8

The gathering for Ralph Stone's funeral was an even sadder affair than the one for his pa two days earlier. Perhaps it was the realization that a young life had been wasted and that Ralph had been a victim as much as his pa and the others. Brannigan had not attended, and when the service ended Thomas headed straight for the sheriff's office. He was intending to bawl out Brannigan for being disrespectful by not attending the funeral, but a shout from across the street had him changing his mind. Jeff Lowrie was still in the specially tailored suit he'd worn at Ralph's funeral. He informed him that Brannigan had arrested a man for the killings, then added:

'We're lucky to have such a fine lawman. I expect you'll be leaving us soon, Marshal Thomas. Perhaps it's best because I understand that you don't have any authority to go around asking questions.'

Thomas didn't like the sly-looking storekeeper, who, he'd heard from more than one person, seemed to think he owned the town. He gave Lowrie one of his glares, but carried on walking.

Thomas was thinking that whoever owned the piebald mare that was hitched alongside Brannigan's horse shouldn't be allowed to keep an animal. The piebald was suffering from severe malnutrition and some form of skin disease. Thomas unbuckled the saddle and dumped it on the ground, then led the animal across the street and hitched it near the water trough.

He was still angry about the state of the animal when he entered the sheriff's office.

'Marshal, I was hoping you'd call in,' greeted Brannigan. 'I managed to catch up with that suspect I was telling you about. Karl Tadcaster's his name and he's back there in the cells.' Brannigan was looking pleased with himself, but

Thomas was in no mood to congratulate him.

'Does that piebald mare outside belong to him?' Thomas snapped struggling to control his anger.

Brannigan acknowledged that it did, and asked why the interest, but Thomas ignored his question and headed for the cells where he found Karl Tadcaster struggling to get off the bed, clearly in some discomfort.

'If you are some kind of legal dude, mister,' Tadcaster said, 'I want Brannigan reported for assault and making trumped-up charges against me.'

Thomas looked Tadcaster up and down as though Tadcaster was a slug that had just crawled from under a stone. Tadcaster was thirty years old; his greasy black hair was brushed back and tied in a pony-tail. He had a look of half-caste Indian about him, with a broad nose and fiery brown eyes and was well dressed for an odd-job man, sporting a black lace shirt with fancy frills on it.

'A man who treats his animal like you do deserves a horse-whipping. I hope Sheriff Brannigan gives you a taste of your own medicine and forgets to feed you.'

Tadcaster grinned at Thomas.

'I like my horses lean and my women well-rounded, but it's none of your dammed business what I do with my animal,' he declared.

Thomas clenched his large fist and snapped at Tadcaster.

'I've just made it my business and if you ever get out of here you won't find that animal, I promise you that. You can come looking for me if you want to make something of it. We'll have a little talk and then I'll rearrange your smarmy face. Now I'm leaving before I ask the sheriff for the keys.'

Karl Tadcaster was thinking that it was time to keep his mouth shut. Whoever the big old guy was, he looked as though he meant business.

'I was going to have the animal put down later,' Brannigan said when

Thomas entered the main office. 'I've heard that Tadcaster is a bit fond of using a whip on his horses.'

'I'll take care of the horse,' Thomas said. 'By the way, the funeral went off all right under the circumstances.'

Brannigan apologized for his absence and said that he hoped that people would understand. Then he added:

'Anyway, I expect you will be moving on soon, now that you have recovered from the shooting. I appreciated your offer to help with the killings, but I hope there's no need now. Tadcaster is linked with all of the killings, and the judge should be here next week. I don't think Tadcaster would have got to ride the piebald again anyhow.'

Thomas was about to disappoint Brannigan when he replied:

'I want to keep an eye on things at the Stones, and I might do a spot of fishing. So I'll be around for a little while yet, and I just hope that my wife will understand. I'll try not to get in your way, but there are a few things that

I would like to check out.'

Brannigan hid his displeasure again as he said:

'What sort of things do you have in mind?'

'I'm not sure exactly. They will probably amount to nothing. Maybe that excuse for a man that you have locked up back there really is responsible for all the killings and that will be the end of it.'

Brannigan frowned.

'If you think that I've got the wrong man, then perhaps you'd better tell me your reasons, Marshal,' he suggested.

'I will, when I think there's something worth telling,' replied Thomas with sufficient abruptness to make Brannigan realize that Thomas wasn't going to share his thoughts on the matter.

Thomas left the sheriff's office and took Tadcaster's horse to the livery. He asked Tad Lawson to feed it up for a few days and to give it a treatment of liniment. Then he headed for the telegraph office.

Thomas had been introduced to the little feller with the thick-rimmed glasses after Josh's funeral and he'd noticed that Seth Crossley seemed to be in a permanent state of nervousness. Thomas wondered if Seth had always had a stutter or if was just recent events that had caused it.

'So, so, so what can I do for you, Marshal?' Crossley asked. Thomas felt guilty for wondering if the messages that Crossley sent contained lots of repeated words. He explained that he wanted some information about the message that had been sent to him by Josh Stone and, in particular, wanted to know if Josh had sent it in person.

Crossley peeled back a few pages of the thick logbook on the desk and then ran his finger down the page.

'Here we are. No, it wasn't Josh. It was Deputy Myers. I remembered him bringing the message in for Josh when you asked me, but I just wanted to be certain.'

'Thanks, Mr Crossley, you've been real helpful. By the way, you might be interested to know that I knew a feller from Montana who had a bit of stammer. The feller's condition was far worse than yours, and he cured it by firing his gun very close to each ear. Of course he was deaf for a little while, but it did the trick, and I'm not kidding. I'd be happy to do it for you if you don't have a weapon of your own.'

'Well, I'm, I'm not sure, sure about that,' Crossley lied. He had no intention of letting the marshal, or anyone else for that matter, fire a gun near his head. It would give him a headache worse than his nagging wife did.

Thomas noticed that Crossley had started blinking and didn't want to stress the man, but he repeated his offer. 'Let me know if you do. I'll be around for a while.'

Thomas had already left the telegraph office by the time Crossley had managed to say: 'Thanks, I will.'

9

Karl Tadcaster's trial opened in the same community hall near the church that Thomas had attended after the funerals. The trial had aroused a good deal of interest because Karl Tadcaster had been dubbed 'the lustful killer'. Some folks were calling it the trial of the century. The town's population had swelled as the trial date approached and a number of reporters from back East had arrived and conducted interviews with Tadcaster. Some had told him that in future years his name would be mentioned alongside Billy the Kid and other notorious characters. Karl Tadcaster lapped up the attention and not being the brightest of men it hadn't occurred to him that he wouldn't be around to enjoy his fame.

Many people, including Brannigan, were claiming that the case against

Tadcaster had been strengthened because the killings had stopped since he'd been arrested, but Thomas still doubted if the little weasel had killed more than one man. Thomas wasn't totally convinced that Brannigan had managed to link the suspect with all the killings. He had a feeling that Tadcaster might end up getting a notoriety that he didn't deserve.

Judge John S Bembridge had given permission for the doors and windows of the community hall to be left open to allow as many folks as possible to witness the trial. If the hall had been six times the size it still wouldn't have accommodated all those who wanted to see the proceedings.

When Thomas had heard that Judge Bembridge had been appointed to preside over the trial he was certain that Tadcaster would be hanged even if he was totally innocent. Thomas had seen Bembridge in action before and witnessed the delight in Bembridge's eyes when he delivered the death sentence. Perhaps all the fifty-two men whom

Bembridge had sentenced to hang had deserved to die, but Thomas doubted it.

Thomas settled himself into his reserved seat just three rows from the judge's table and glanced around the packed hall to see if Barbara Stone had changed her mind about not attending. Only a small number of women were present and he was glad that she wasn't amongst them.

Judge Bembridge's jowly face was as fierce as his reputation as he poured himself a whiskey from the bottle on the desk and then called the court to order. Bembridge was sixty-two years old, five foot six and needed specially tailored suits to accommodate his wide girth. His liking for food nearly matched his liking for whiskey. The face still bore the scars of a severe beating that he'd received at the hands of the kinfolk of a man he'd sentenced to hang. The broken cheekbone had never healed properly, but the beating had not affected his draconian treatment of those brought before him or his habit of misguiding the jury. He took another slug of whiskey to clear his throat and then opened the proceedings.

'Before I ask Mr Farley to outline the case against the accused I would remind the court that the defendant has been charged with killing four men, but I don't intend to read out the full names of Beamish, Norris, Stone and Cutler. I have read Sheriff Brannigan's supporting evidence and I propose that the defendant is tried for the murder of Jack Beamish, the first man whom he was accused of killing.' While Bembridge paused to have another slug of whiskey, the prosecutor, Mort Farley and the defence counsel, Edward Hoskins went into a huddle.

'Is there a problem, gentlemen?' Bembridge directed his question at the legal men. The men looked at each other, surprised by the directness of the question. Farley and Hoskins could have been brothers, both thirty years old, six foot tall, clean cut and immaculately dressed in their dark suits.

'No, sir,' Farley replied for them both. 'We were just clarifying a point of law, but we have resolved it now, thank you.' The two men had actually been discussing whether Bembridge would have to be carried out at the end of the trial if he continued drinking at the present rate.

'Good,' Bembridge snapped. 'The defendant can only be hanged once, although I daresay that there are some folks present here who would like the fornicating killer to hang four times, but I regret to say that's not possible. However, if there are any special reasons for referring to the other cases by way of helping either counsel, then I may accept references to them. I must warn you, gentlemen, that I can't abide lawyers who like the sound of their own voices, especially if it means that this case isn't wrapped up before my belly starts to rumble.'

Thomas studied Tadcaster's reaction while Farley outlined the case against him, and concluded that Tadcaster was dumber than he looked, perhaps relishing his reputation as a man who liked women. The smile on Tadcaster's face broadened when it was claimed that he had fathered at least twelve children, a feat that was at least matched by his pa who'd been knifed to death by a jealous woman. Karl Tadcaster had once been shot in the leg by an irate husband and in the buttocks by a protective father, but this had not dampened his sexual appetite.

Tadcaster agreed under cross-examination by Farley that he had done some work at the Beamish property and had been involved in a row with Jack Beamish over his wife. He also agreed that Beamish had threatened that he would make sure that Tadcaster never worked in, or near Letana Creek ever again. Tadcaster grinned before he recalled Beamish's last threat.

'Beamish said that he would cut my balls off, but he wasn't the first husband of a pleasure-seeking wife to say that to me. Most of those cowboy suckers work too hard and don't save enough energy for the bedroom.' Hoskins wished that Judge Bembridge would silence his client, but the judge seemed quite happy to let Tadcaster talk himself into trouble.

By the time that Farley had finished outlining the case against Tadcaster, he had established that there was motive, and he reminded the court that Tadcaster could not provide any evidence of his whereabouts at the time Beamish was murdered.

During Hoskin's cross-examination of Tadcaster he tried to develop the idea that Tadcaster liked women, but only those who were available. He wasn't pleased when Tadcaster added the rider: 'or willing'. The only reference that Hoskins made to the other killings was when he asked Tadcaster if he had ever worked for Josh Stone or made any advances towards Shelley Stone.

'I only did a small job for Stone and never made a move on the women, but that girl Shelley sure is a beauty and her ma isn't exactly a dog. I wouldn't say no to either of them, but I never got the chance. I remember that Stone wasn't too pleased when I was chatting to them both in town one day. He threatened me as well, just because I was sweet-talking two pretty women. I only told them what they were missing in bed. Now is that a crime?' Tadcaster grinned at the jury.

Hoskins looked skywards before declaring: 'No further questions.' He was on his way to his seat when Tadcaster called after him.

'Ain't you going to ask where I was when Beamish was shot?'

Hoskins looked flustered. 'You've already testified that you can't remember,' he replied.

'Well, now I can,' Tadcaster declared, clearly enjoying the occasion. 'I spent the whole afternoon in bed with Avril Booth while her old man was away at some Bible convention thing at Clearwater Valley.' The court room was filled with chatter and Myrtle Crossley was still delivering her declaration that she never did trust that woman, when everyone else had responded to the sound of Judge Bembridge's gavel striking the desk. The newspaper men scribbled away like fury, safe in the knowledge that their journey hadn't been wasted.

Hoskins recovered from his despair and asked for an adjournment, to which Judge Bembridge responded by staggering to his feet and announced that the court was adjourned for thirty minutes. Bembridge needed to find the location of the nearest ablutions and obtain a fresh bottle of whiskey. Hoskins had the briefest of conversations with Tadcaster and then asked Sheriff Brannigan to fetch Avril Booth, adding that it might be a good idea if he informed the Reverend Booth about the developments.

★ ★ ★

The Reverend Booth was standing in the pulpit, practising his sermon, and his wife was arranging flowers when Brannigan entered the church.

The preacher frowned, clearly upset that Brannigan was still armed, and called out to him that there was no place for instruments of death in the house of the Lord.

'I'm sorry, Reverend, but I'm kind of in a hurry and I'd like a word with you and your good lady. Perhaps we could all go outside.'

The Reverend Booth looked annoyed and his wife looked worried. Once they were outside, Brannigan didn't mince his words and told them exactly what Tadcaster had claimed in court. The minister's countenance had changed from annoyance to rage.

'The man must be sick or perverted to suggest such a thing. I would have expected you to have dismissed it as nonsense and not had the effrontery to embarrass us in this way.'

Brannigan sighed. 'I can understand how you feel, Reverend, but a man's life is at stake, and I'm duty-bound to follow up his claims.'

The minister managed to restore some of his composure before he spoke.

'Of course you are, and I'm sorry for my outburst. Now if you'll excuse us, Sheriff, we have things to do.' He hoped that that was the end of the matter, but then his wife spoke in what was almost a whisper.

'It's true.'

'What did you say, dear?' he asked, screwing his thin face up in irritation.

Avril Booth lifted her head and spoke much louder this time.

'I said it's true. What the sheriff said about Karl Tadcaster and me is true.'

'Don't be silly, Avril. You can't save Karl Tadcaster from damnation just by lying for him. Now let's go back inside the church and finish our work and stop wasting the sheriff's time.'

She ignored her husband as she spoke directly to Brannigan.

'Will I need to give evidence, Sheriff?'

He was taken aback by her confession, but he had no doubt that she was telling the truth.

'I'm afraid so, Mrs Booth. You'll need to come back to the hall and speak to Edward Hoskins who is defending Tadcaster. The trial is due to restart shortly and I'm certain you'll be called as a witness.'

Avril Booth was no longer looking worried. She was an honest lady and a brave one.

'Then I'm ready to come with you,' she said, simply.

Brannigan asked the minister if he was coming to give his wife support.

The minister glowered at Brannigan before he replied.

'Why would I want to offer this self-confessed sinner my support?' He spoke as though his wife wasn't there as he continued: 'You can tell her that her belongings will be outside the front door of my house when she's finished in court. Perhaps she might want to stay with the other whores at the saloon tonight.' He turned and headed back towards the church without looking at his wife. Brannigan shook his head, bemused by the reaction of the Bible-puncher.

'The reverend doesn't exactly practise what he preaches. I wonder what happened to all that understanding and forgiveness he talks about.'

During the short walk back to the hall, Brannigan told Avril Booth to ignore any tittle-tattle that might come from the onlookers in the court. He hoped that his advice might help, because he felt sorry for her.

Judge Bembridge was already seated and there was a fresh bottle of whiskey on the desk. Brannigan noted that even more bodies had squeezed into the tightly packed courtroom. Thomas was the only person who did not turn to look at Avril Booth and soon the air was full of loud mutterings, mainly from the women. Bembridge's gavel thumped against the desk once more, startling many of the spectators and a member of the jury who had dozed off, but then silence descended once more. Bembridge wasn't going to let them off with just a mild warning this time.

'I know the females of the species have great difficulty in managing to keep their tongues in the rest position for very long. But if there are any more outbursts I'll ask the sheriff to remove anyone who is wearing a dress from this court, except the witness of course.'

While the judge was issuing his warning, Edward Hoskins had been in a deep conversation with Avril Booth. He had managed to brief her about court procedures by the time that Judge Bembridge asked him if he was ready to proceed.

'I am, sir, and I would like to call Mrs Avril Booth to the stand as a witness for the defence.'

Avril Booth eased her plump frame into the narrow chair. Her cheeks were normally rosy, but now they positively glowed. She pushed the dark-brown hair from her face and stared directly at Edward Hoskins, just as he had instructed her to.

'Mrs Booth, can you tell the court if you can remember where you were on the afternoon that Jack Beamish was murdered.'

She replied in a firm voice that she was at home all afternoon.

'Was anyone else with you during that time, and if so can you tell the court who it was?'

Avril Booth turned her eyes towards the smirking Tadcaster and replied:

'Karl Tadcaster was with me all afternoon.'

Myrtle Crossley's mouth opened, but she managed to stop herself crying out, as did the other women.

Against all the odds it looked as though Tadcaster's life might have been saved, but a brave woman's reputation had just been ruined.

'So, Karl Tadcaster couldn't have killed Jack Beamish that day. You're certain that he was with you all afternoon?' Hoskins asked her to confirm.

She nodded her head in agreement and when asked to give a clear answer, she did so in a quiet but firm voice.

Hoskins hated asking the next question, but he had no choice.

'How can you be so sure? Where were you exactly?'

When she replied that they were in bed all afternoon, the women folk couldn't hold themselves back. Bembridge was refilling his glass at the time and let the outburst die down without carrying out his threat to banish them from the court. Hoskins was about to ask for the case against Tadcaster to be dismissed when Avril Booth spoke again.

'But Karl did kill Luke Cutler,' she said calmly.

Hoskins was anxious to get Avril Booth off the stand before Farley declared her an unreliable witness. 'No further questions, Mrs Booth. You may stand down.'

Judge Bembridge had given the impression that his thoughts had been elsewhere while Avril Booth was giving her evidence, but he had absorbed every word. He asked her to stay seated and to explain her accusation about the murder of Luke Cutler.

Thomas could have punched the air with satisfaction when he'd heard Avril Booth's declaration, because it had solved one of his doubts. Luke Cutler was only twenty-five years old, but the other victims had all been well over fifty, and they had other things in common that they didn't share with Cutler. It also explained why Josh Stone had only referred to two killings in his letter when there had been three at the time.

Avril Booth told the court that on the day that Luke Cutler died she had arranged to meet Karl Tadcaster in the small barn at his grandma's place, but he was an hour late. When he arrived, he confessed that he'd killed Luke Cutler. He made her promise that if the sheriff came looking for him, she would say that she was visiting his old and confused grandma all afternoon, and that Tadcaster was there with them.

Judge Bembridge was clearly impressed by her testimony and thanked Avril Booth for her courage. He told her that he excluded her from his previous comments about the female sex and added that she was a very special lady. Then he turned his gaze in the direction of the women seated near the front and noted with satisfaction that they were bristling with indignation and embarrassment.

Judge Bembridge continued in his unorthodox style when he asked the foreman of the jury, Jeff Lowrie, if they had any need to retire or were they agreed that Avril Booth was a reliable witness. He added that if the jury accepted her as a reliable witness then they must find Karl Tadcaster guilty of murdering Luke Cutler.

Jeff Lowrie was taken aback by the abruptness of the question, but several of the jury had already nodded in response to it, making their views clear. Within seconds Lowrie confirmed the verdict that Bembridge had already guided them towards.

'Then we have a satisfactory result,' Bembridge declared, then told Tadcaster to stand and remain silent while the sentence was announced. Karl Tadcaster was no longer smiling after Judge Bembridge sentenced him to death by hanging.

Tadcaster's ranting plea of innocence and accusations that Avril Booth was a madwoman could not be heard above the uproar in the court. Judge Bembridge announced that the case was closed, but this time the gavel was not raised, only the glass towards his mouth.

Thomas offered to assist Brannigan with Tadcaster, who was still ranting and cursing. The sheriff declined the offer but suggested that Avril Booth was in need of some help because her husband had made her homeless. Thomas always felt uncomfortable in these situations, but he put a comforting arm around Avril Booth and shepherded her out of the court. He had intended to take her to the hotel, but when he saw Barbara and Shelley Stone across the street he guided her in the direction of the wagon which they were sitting on. He briefly covered what had happened in court and when he explained that Avril Booth was homeless, Barbara insisted that Mrs Booth stay with her and Shelley.

10

There had been no burial ceremony for Karl Tadcaster following his hanging, just an unmarked grave, but there was no shortage of interest when folks attended church the following Sunday. The church hall was full in the expectation of a torrent of hell and damnation from the Reverend Booth. It was the first time that Barbara Stone had missed a church service apart from when she had been unable to attend through illness, but she had preferred to stay at home and comfort Avril Booth.

Avril Booth was not inclined to exaggeration and Barbara believed her tales of the brutality that her husband had inflicted on her over the years. He had often banished his wife from the marital bed, claiming that God wanted them to forgo pleasure to make them appreciate what others never had. She had learned never to pay any man the slightest compliment because her husband would react with rage once they were alone.

The minister did not disappoint those who had gathered for his anticipated ranting when he declared that Karl Tadcaster had been a follower of the Devil. Some of the congregation sniggered when he preached that some men are weak when it comes to pleasures of the flesh. Man needed to control his natural urges of desire even though for some it was a constant battle. But women could not blame nature for their evil. God had intended that a woman should be faithful to one man. Woman was designed to give pleasure and not receive it herself. Those who sought pleasure and strayed into the arms of another man were daughters of the Devil.

As the church service was nearing its end, the minister read out a selection of letters that he had received. The first two were very similar, and offered him sympathy for the way that his wife had humiliated him and sinned in the eyes of God.

'I'm touched by the kindness relayed to me in the letters. It means so much to me,' he explained. 'I would just like to read one more then we can all go and do the good Lord's work.' He faltered as he started to read the letter, and continued to read it in silence until he stopped, and then he scanned the congregation, anxious to identify the writer of the letter. His eyes settled on the three women just a couple of rows from the front, and the blood drained from his face. He usually greeted every member of the congregation as they entered the church, but today he had broken with the custom because there had been so many worshippers. None of the three saloon-girls had ever attended the church before, and it was unlikely that they would ever attend again.

Booth made a mumbled apology before hurrying away into the little room to the side of the pulpit. When he hadn't returned five minutes later the three women stood up and started to make their way out of the church. Melanie declared in a loud voice that the lecherous old devil probably wouldn't be coming back, and they had likely just lost one of their best customers. Emily and Meryl followed Melanie's announcement with a chorus of: 'But we won't be missing him.'

Some of the men looked on in amusement at the antics of the saloon girls whilst their womenfolk were clearly shocked. None of the congregation would ever know the full contents of the letter that the girls had sent the hypocritical minister, but most could have guessed. Letana Creek would need a new minister, and Avril Booth would soon be moving back into her old house.

*   *   *

Thomas smiled when he heard about the saloon girls' escapade in the church, but he wasn't amused two nights later when he spotted Cliff Myers leaving Melanie's room at the hotel. Judging by the way they'd parted, Myers hadn't been there on any official business. Thomas intended to read the riot act to Myers, but before then there were some more serious concerns about Myers that had been playing on his mind, including the question of whether Ralph Stone's suicide had been faked by his killer. Myers had certainly had the opportunity. It was either him or Brannigan, even though neither man appeared to have a motive, at least none that Thomas could fathom. It still bothered him that Myers looked strangely familiar and yet their paths had never crossed.

It was three days from the deadline Thomas had set himself before he would leave Letana Creek, when he called on Brannigan to enquire if there had been any developments with the investigation into the other killings.

Brannigan shook his head.

'I don't see how we are going to find out anything new unless someone else gets killed,' replied Brannigan. 'I was just telling Myers that I might have to lay him off soon or maybe have him work part-time.'

'It couldn't come at a worse time for me because I was planning on asking Shelley to marry me,' said Myers.

The mention of marriage, and so soon after all the upset didn't go down well with Thomas and he made his feelings known to Myers.

'You won't save money by spending it on the saloon-girls like Melanie. You remember — at the hotel, just the other night?'

Myers was annoyed with himself for being so careless that he had been seen by the marshal, but was confident that he could talk his way out of trouble.

'I'm not proud of that, Marshal, but Shelley's a churchgoing girl and it's difficult having to wait. You must remember what it's like having to resist such things, especially with a beautiful girl like Shelley.'

Thomas was in no mood to let Myers wriggle out of this. 'If that's supposed to be an excuse,' he said, 'then it's a feeble one for someone who is thinking of marriage. I'll give you until this time tomorrow to tell Shelley what you've been up to, otherwise I'll tell her.'

Myers's face reddened.

'What happens between me and Shelley is none of your goddam business, Marshal,' Myers retorted.

'I'm making it my business. Josh Stone didn't like you, Myers, and I think I understand why.' Then, as an afterthought, Thomas asked a question that had been bothering him. 'Did you read the telegram that Josh asked you to send me about a week before he died?'

'I didn't have to,' Myers answered. 'Josh told me he was sending for you. He said that he wanted your help, but didn't give any details, and no, I didn't read the message.'

Brannigan was surprised by the

heated exchange. It appeared that Thomas's upset with Myers wasn't just about his being an unsuitable suitor for an old friend's daughter.

'Cliff may be a young fool with the women, Marshal, and it'll land him in trouble one day, but it seems you're suggesting he's done something more serious. Although I'm a bit puzzled myself as to why Cliff didn't tell me you'd been sent for.' Brannigan looked at Myers, inviting him to explain, but all he got was a sheepish look and a less than convincing:

'Sorry, Sheriff. I must have forgotten about it.'

Thomas looked Myers in the eye. 'While we're getting things out in the open,' he said, 'I think Ralph Stone was murdered and his killer made it look like suicide.'

Myers rounded on Thomas.

'So that's what this is all about. I suppose you think that I did it because I gave him the knife.'

'If Ralph Stone was murdered, and

I'm not saying that he definitely was,' replied Thomas, 'then probably only you and the sheriff had the opportunity. I saw the sheriff return here when I was walking back to the hotel after the funeral and he wouldn't have had time to kill Ralph. So that just leaves you.'

Myers was clearly angry and agitated by the accusation.

'So you really are accusing me! Well, I've had enough of this. I'm leaving right now unless Sheriff Brannigan intends to arrest me.'

Brannigan couldn't see how Thomas could justify his accusation and entered the dispute with some questions of his own.

'That's pretty strong stuff, Marshal. Why would Myers want to kill Ralph when the two boys got on so well? What sort of motive would he have?'

Thomas knew that the accusation was flimsy, and despite all his experience he might just have played his hand against Myers too soon.

'The truth is, I don't know what the

motive was, but I can tell you why it wasn't suicide.' Thomas explained how the one word message scrawled in Ralph's blood couldn't have been his own work.

Myers shook his head in mock disbelief.

'And that's all you've got. Perhaps Ralph didn't kill himself, but I can prove to you that it wasn't me and make you look a damned fool.'

Thomas was shaken by the confidence of Myers' declaration and was anxious to hear the reply when Brannigan asked Myers how he could prove Thomas was wrong.

'Because when I brought Ralph back to the cell after his pa's funeral Shelley was with me. I locked the office and then we both went back to the church hall. I was with her until I came back here and found you both in Ralph's cell.'

Brannigan suggested that it would be a simple thing to verify, but he would have to lock him up until Thomas had checked out Myers' story with Shelley.

On the ride out to the Stone Ranch Thomas was regretting accusing Myers the way he had, but he would have to go through with it now and hope that it wouldn't upset the Stones too much. He didn't intend to reveal his theory about Ralph's death to them, unless he had to.

Barbara Stone was looking better now that the redness around her eyes had gone. Perhaps helping Avril Booth had made her forget her own troubles, but Thomas knew from his own experience that she would be feeling lonely for a long time, missing the little things that she and Josh had done together.

'I hope you don't mind me calling on you again,' he apologized when she had welcomed him in. He couldn't see Shelley so there was a chance that his journey had been wasted. 'It's just that I have a few loose ends that I wanted to clear up about the killings and Shelley might be able to help me with one of them, but it's not that important.'

Barbara told him that he would find Shelley in the barn grooming her horse. She offered to prepare him some coffee and food while he went to see her daughter.

His chat with Shelley turned out to be more difficult than he'd expected, but at least he managed to get some answers from her and his trip certainly hadn't been wasted.

* * *

When Thomas returned to town he headed straight for Brannigan's office for another confrontation with Myers, but not before he told Brannigan about his chat with Shelley. He explained that Shelley was clearly besotted with Myers but she had been upset to learn that Myers was two-timing her. She had also revealed that she had been giving Ralph secret lessons and that he had learned to read and write. Ralph had been planning to surprise his pa with his new-found skills, but never got the chance. And she had backed up Myers's story about their being together at the time that Ralph had died.

'Well, there's no real harm been done,' said Brannigan, trying to comfort Thomas. 'I must admit that I thought you were out of line suspecting Myers, but then again I know him a lot better than you do. I'll go and get him, and I expect you'll want to put things right.'

Thomas hadn't really changed his mind about Myers, but when he apologized to him he discovered that Myers was in no mood for forgiving. He spurned the apology.

'I can do better than this town, but before I leave I'll tell Shelley that it's your fault, Marshal.'

'But there's no need for you to leave town, Myers, now that everything's been cleared up,' suggested Thomas. Myers wasn't about to take the olive branch, and he snapped at Thomas once again.

'I've told you that I've had it with this place, but there are always fresh challenges when you're young, so don't worry about me, old man.'

Myers offered his hand to Brannigan.

'Thanks for everything, Sheriff. I enjoyed working with a proper lawman and not one who should have been put out to grass a long time ago. Be lucky, Sheriff.'

Brannigan and Thomas watched Myers leave the office and then Thomas smiled ruefully.

'I guess I deserved some of that,' he said.

11

Thomas accepted that with the collapse of his case against Myers he was chasing a lost cause. He was no quitter, but he was a realist and it was time to return home to Statton Crossing and Olive. Brannigan seemed to be a good enough lawman, despite his inexperience and perhaps he would get lucky and find the killer one day. That was if the killer wasn't already dead. Perhaps it was Tadcaster after all.

Thomas had said his goodbyes to the folks in town the night before, settled his bills and left a supply of whiskey for Doc Schultz. It suddenly felt like a long time ago when he'd come around and seen the wizened face of the old doc.

He planned to bring Olive to see Barbara Stone one day, but he couldn't leave Letana Creek without visiting the graveyard to say farewell to his old friend.

Barbara Stone was already at the cemetery entrance, as arranged, when he got there. Thomas removed his hat and linked arms with her as they made their way to where Josh and Ralph were buried. As Barbara laid the small sheaf of fresh flowers, Thomas stood with his head bowed. He said a silent 'Goodbye, friend' and took a step back before telling Barbara that he would leave her alone while he strolled around the cemetery.

'Thank you,' she whispered to the man who had become a good friend and a pillar of strength in her time of need. She had welcomed his help more easily than that of friends whom she had known for a very long time. Perhaps he reminded her of Josh, because they were similar in some ways. She knew that he'd lived a life of violence, but he had a caring and protective way that made her feel safe and secure.

Thomas managed to weave his way carefully amongst the graves, pausing to read the details of those laid to rest. The recent burials had all been close to the Stones' graves, but he felt drawn to a grave at the far side of the cemetery, which was in a section where most of the crosses were broken. The grave that had caught his attention was well maintained, and there was a large display of flowers on it. The inscription on the cross was faded, but still readable.

ROBERT LEO SHACKLADE
Born 1835 — Died 1860

A piece of fresh wood nailed near the base of the cross had the message '*Shot in the back by cowards*' and it must have been added recently.

Thomas was startled by the voice of Barbara Stone who had come to join him.

'So you found the mystery grave,' she said. Thomas turned to face her. 'It does stand out amongst the others, but what's the mystery?'

'There isn't one really. It's just that the grave was neglected like the others nearby until about a month ago when flowers started appearing, and that piece of wood with the chilling message was placed there. Ever since then the flowers have been changed regularly, but now those look a bit jaded.'

Thomas was intrigued.

'And no one has ever seen who attends the grave?' he asked.

'I'm not sure if anyone else has, but Josh did. It was just a few weeks before he died. He was delivering some produce to town very early one morning when he saw the person kneeling down by the grave.'

Thomas's mind was getting ahead of itself when he asked, 'Then you know who it is?'

Barbara Stone smiled at the memory of her husband.

'I'm afraid I don't. Josh felt that it wouldn't be right to reveal the identity because the man clearly wanted it to be kept a secret. I told him that I wouldn't tell him the town gossip unless he told me who it was, not that Josh was one for gossip. It was just our little joke.'

At least she had revealed that Josh had let it slip that the person was a man. Thomas was disappointed when she answered his questions, telling him that there were no Shacklades still living in the town and she knew nothing about the buried man's death.

By the time that Thomas had escorted Barbara back to her wagon he had decided to postpone his departure by a couple of days.

'Is it something to do with that grave and the killings?' she asked after he told her about his change of plans.

'I'm thinking that there could be a link, even though it happened such a long time ago. I'd like to check a few things out, but I expect anyone who could provide information is either dead or will have moved on. It's probably best if you don't mention this to anyone, Barbara.'

Thomas returned to town, but he wouldn't be telling Brannigan about his theory that the murders might be some sort of revenge for a killing that had taken place more than a couple of decades ago, at least not yet. He had been made to look foolish over his claims about Ralph's death, and he didn't want to risk it happening again. All the men had been shot in the back, just like Robert Shacklade, but he reminded himself that it was the most common way that men died from gunshot wounds. Not in face-to-face gunfights, as some of the folks back East imagined, or like it was portrayed in story books.

It was probably just a coincidence that the killings began shortly after the flowers had started appearing on the grave, but there was still the possibility that Josh Stone was dead just because he happened to see someone in a graveyard early one morning.

Thomas booked back into the hotel and told the man on reception there had been a change of plans. Thomas didn't elaborate when he told Brannigan the same thing later.

After seeing Brannigan, he bought a bottle of whiskey at the store, then headed for the saloon and the two old-timers who were sitting in the shade on wooden seats near the entrance. Thomas didn't know how old Jake Stookey and Matty Conlan were and he wouldn't like to guess, but when he placed the bottle of whiskey close to their seat, he was fairly certain that these two were the oldest men in town by a wide margin.

'Howdy, gents, I was hoping that you might help me with a bit of local history, and I've brought along something for your trouble.'

Matty Conlon eyed him suspiciously.

'What does he want? Is he trying to sell us some whiskey? Tell him we ain't got any money.'

Jake matched his friend's delivery of

spit when he leaned over and shouted in his ear:

'It's the old marshal. He wants to have a chinwag.'

Conlan screwed up his face in puzzlement.

'He doesn't look like a marshal. He looks even older than you, Jake.'

Thomas had already decided that he wasn't going to get much help from Matty, but at least he had a chance with Jake.

'There ain't any use you asking Matty anything, Marshal, unless you intend the whole of the town to hear. He's deaf in both ears. He claims that it was caused by cannon fire, but it might be on account that his ears are strangers to water. I remember seeing a bean drop out of one of them one day.' Jake cackled at the memory, puffed on his clay pipe and then addressed Thomas. 'Fire away with your questions, Marshal, and I'll do my best to help you.'

Thomas explained that he was trying

to trace any surviving members of Robert Shacklade's family, who once lived in Letana Creek.

Jake didn't react to the name, but stroked his chin and then ruffled his thatch of snowy-white hair that hadn't seen a brush for as long as Matty's ears hadn't seen water.

'Shacklade, Shacklade,' Jake repeated while he tried to jog his memory. 'There ain't anyone goes by that name lives here now, I can tell you that. The name sure sounds familiar though, but I don't know why.' He turned and shouted into Matty's ear, asking him if he knew any Shacklades.

Matty grinned.

'I sure do,' he shouted. 'Mary Shacklade had a pair of titties like ripe plums. She lived over towards Zukon Pass, but I haven't seen her for years. I wonder if she could still make an oldie like me come to life in bed.'

Jake shook his head.

'I think he means melons, and the woman he remembers was a Mary

Shackelton.' Jake suddenly clicked his fingers. 'I've got it. There was a lot of talk recently about a grave in the cemetery belonging to someone called Shacklade. I knew I'd heard the name, but you'd need to find someone who was around at the time the feller died. Matty was here then, but his memory isn't too good. I came here about twenty years ago just after the drought, but a lot of the original families left about that time.'

Thomas was encouraged when Jake suggested that if he didn't mind a ride out of town there was a man who would be worth talking to.

'He was a lawman, just like you, and he should be able to help. That's if his home-made whiskey, or what he puts in his pipe hasn't scrambled his brains by now.'

Thomas listened carefully while Jake gave him the directions to the homestead of retired Sheriff Todd Brewer, then he bid the odd pair farewell. He was some distance away when he heard

Matty shout out:

'Who was that ugly, one-eyed feller you were talking to?'

★ ★ ★

It was mid-afternoon when Thomas reached the faded signpost that pointed to Meo Valley mine, where he hoped to find the home of old Todd Brewer. It wasn't long before the trail became so overgrown that Thomas was thinking that either he was lost or old Jake had sent him on a wildgoose chase. The stallion was beginning to show signs of disapproval at having to force his way through the undergrowth, and he was getting spooked by the movement of wildlife, including snakes that were slithering away after being disturbed. Thomas was on the verge of turning back when he came out into a clearing and he saw the tiny cabin ahead. The sight of the neat fence around the property brought a smile to his face. It wasn't likely that Brewer would suffer from disputes with neighbours or trespassers out here, but he guessed the old sheriff was like most folks, and territorial by nature. The property looked as though it might still be occupied, judging by its condition and the large number of chickens that were clearly startled by his arrival. He dismounted and led the stallion to the water-trough, but changed his mind when he got a whiff of the stale water. He secured the horse to the porch way rail.

As he approached the open front door, he called out:

'Anyone at home?'

Then he remembered old Matty's deafness and called out again, but much louder this time. Thinking that the old feller might be having his afternoon siesta, Thomas edged his way inside and a familiar smell hit his nostrils. It was a smell to which Thomas was no stranger. It was the smell of death. He cupped a hand over his mouth and nose before he ventured inside the cabin. The squealing of the rats stopped as they scurried away. There was an empty whiskey bottle on the table, next to the chair where a decomposed body lay. He assumed it was Todd Brewer, but whoever the poor soul was, he'd been dead for a very long time. Thomas moved the chair to face towards the light causing the occupant to fall to the floor, sending up a cloud of dust. He shook his head and smiled when he saw a sheriff's badge pinned to the crumpled, faded shirt on the corpse. It was a safe bet that it was Todd Brewer, and it was likely that he had died from natural causes or maybe whiskey poisoning.

Thomas's search for some documents that might help him was unsuccessful, but he did find a bundle of faded Wanted posters. They all had a large pencil tick on the top right-hand corner. Thomas wondered whether they might have been posters of men whom Brewer had arrested.

He considered setting fire to the

cabin with Brewer inside, but feared that he might start a forest fire. When he later discovered the two wooden crosses in the ground under the hanging branches of what looked like an apple-tree, he was glad that he hadn't cremated the remains of Todd Brewer. One cross bore the words: *Nelly Brewer — My Wife. Born 1812 — Died 1881* and the other one: *Sheriff Todd Brewer. Born 1810 Died?* Todd Brewer had even prepared his own grave. After ferreting around, Thomas found a shovel in the tiny shed and set about digging out Brewer's grave. The ground was soft enough and he soon reached a reasonable depth. He pulled Brewer's cross from the ground and used his Bowie knife to inscribe last year's date of 1885 over the faint question mark put there by Brewer. He was fairly certain that if he tried to move Brewer's remains they would fall apart, so he laid a blanket beside them and he soon had the skeleton bundled inside it. It wasn't the most dignified way for a man to be carried to his final resting place, but at least he was still in one piece.

After filling in the grave he was feeling the effects of his recent gunshot wound and was puffing hard, thinking perhaps he should reduce his pipe-smoking. He remembered one doctor telling him that smoking was real bad for you, but Thomas told him that his grandpa had smoked a pipe since he was ten years old and he'd lived until he was eighty-six. He'd died from a snake-bite and not on account of smoking.

Thomas wasn't a religious man, but the rosary beads and the Bible in the cabin indicated that the Brewers had probably been God-fearing folks. He wasn't very good with words, but with only the chickens and rats listening, he wasn't going to be criticized for the few words he spoke as he stood over the graves.

He was saddened by the demise of Brewer because it would have been interesting, swapping tales about their lives as lawmen.

Thomas was tempted to close the cabin door before he left, but figured that it provided some shelter for the chickens, which had no doubt grown in number since the loss of their master.

★   ★   ★

He took his time on the journey back to Letana Creek, once again mulling over recent events and thinking about Olive back in Statton Crossing, worrying about him. By the time he reached town he had decided that he would be heading for home in the morning, but before then he had a plan that might just help catch the killer. He would put the plan into operation tonight, but first, he would write a very important letter.

Thomas intended to try and flush out the killer, who, he was still convinced, must be connected with the killing of Robert Shacklade. He didn't know how, but he would bet all that he owned that it did. It might be a revengeful relative, assuming that Shacklade had one. It might be someone who was frightened of being identified as Shacklade's killer even after the passing of so many years. He had dismissed the idea that the flowers had been laid by someone who had developed a guilty conscience that might have been triggered by the first back-shooting. Thomas was hoping that the killer would fear that his identity was going to be revealed by Brewer, but Thomas would need to convince the killer that Sheriff Brewer was still alive.

It was early evening when Thomas slipped the letter under the door of the telegraph office with a note for Seth Crossley, and then made his way to the saloon. The last time he had visited the drinking-house the atmosphere had been sombre, but tonight the place was buzzing. Perhaps folks were beginning to relax now that the killings had stopped. One of the saloon-girls gave him a smile, but she was just being friendly and not touting for business. He hadn't been introduced to many folks, except a few close friends of the Stones, but his reputation had spread, and he received a few friendly nods on his way to the bar. Some believed that he had killed twenty-two men which was nearly double the officially recorded figure and he had certainly earned their respect in the short time that he had been there.

'The first drink's free tonight, Marshal, so what it'll be?' asked the barman, who was a cheerful feller who, Thomas had a feeling, could handle himself. He hadn't got that flattened nose and rough hands just by serving drinks.

'I'll have a beer and I'll pay for a whiskey,' Thomas replied. The barman poured the drinks and pushed them across the counter.

'I'd heard that you'd left our quaint little town, Marshall,' he remarked.

Thomas gulped down the whiskey

and pushed the empty glass back towards the barman, indicating that he wanted a refill.

'I was meant to have left today, but I've discovered something important concerning the recent killings.'

'Most folks still think the killings were down to Tadcaster,' said the surprised barman.

'Tadcaster only killed one man and tomorrow I aim to prove it, with a little help from Todd Brewer, the old town sheriff.'

The barman passed back the refilled glass and took Thomas's money off the counter.

'I've never heard the name Brewer,' he said. 'Must have been before my time.'

Joe Dalton, who helped out at Lowrie's store, sidled closer to Thomas.

'I don't think Brewer will be able to help you, Marshal,' Dalton advised. 'He ain't been in town for a very long time. He must have died by now. Anyway, how could he have helped you?'

Thomas turned to face Dalton.

'Well he wasn't dead when I spoke to him today. He promised to help me solve the mystery of the recent killings if I delivered him four bottles of whiskey and some baccy tomorrow. He told me that the killings were linked to what happened to Robert Shacklade a long time ago. Shacklade was shot in the back by someone from this town and he's buried up on the hill. Someone's been attending his grave while the killings have been going on.'

A few men had edged closer to Thomas, eager to hear more of what the marshal had to say.

'What you mean, all those killings were to do with revenge because of what happened to this Robert Shacklade?' asked Dalton.

'Revenge could have been the motive, or it could have been someone who was connected to his killing. He might have wanted to silence those who knew something about Shacklade's death. My feeling is that some innocent men got killed, including my friend Josh Stone.'

'So what do you aim to do, Marshal?' asked one of the gathering.

'I'm going to ride out to Brewer's place just after sun-up, and by this time tomorrow the killer will be in a cell across the road waiting to hang.'

Thomas had picked up his third whiskey before he moved away from the bar, leaving Joe Dalton and the group still engaged in a discussion about the killings. The plan was developing just like he hoped it would. With luck the word would spread to the man it was intended for. The killer might even be in the bar at this very moment and have heard it already. Joe Dalton was about the right age!

When Thomas edged his way over to the card-game he was surprised to see Cliff Myers was one of the players. Their eyes met at the same time, and Myers' were filled with hate.

'Well, if it isn't old one-eye,' Myers mocked. 'I would have thought you were keeping the widow Stone company. The poor man's hardly cold and you've been sniffing around like a randy cowpoke who's just off a cattle drive.' Thomas's instinct was to whip the foul-mouthed upstart, but he didn't want anything to get in the way of his plans for tomorrow, so he walked on. The saloon was noisy, but he still heard the chair being scraped on the floor, signalling to him that Myers had stood up.

'Heh, grandpa, don't walk away from me when I'm talking to you.'

Thomas stopped and turned around to face the advancing Myers.

'Why don't you go back to your game, son? You'll stand more chance of winning at cards than what you're trying to start here. Your face is too pretty to have been in a proper brawl. Why don't you keep it that way?'

Thomas hadn't meant it to be funny, but there was a chorus of laughter from those nearby.

'The old feller intends to give you a

good whippin', Myers. Best do as he says and sit down, pretty boy,' one of the card-players jokingly advised.

'I ain't sitting down until I've given this ugly son of a bitch a good thrashing for sticking his great fat nose into my business. Shelley Stone finished with me today because of him. He should have stayed in his rocking-chair instead of coming here and interfering in things.'

Myers picked up a bottle and struck it against the hard table, but it didn't break and before he could try again, Thomas butted him on the bridge of his nose. Myers staggered back, but stayed on his feet. The bottle had fallen from his hand and as he reached for his pistol Thomas butted him again. This time the hard bone of Thomas's forehead struck Myers' nose and mouth, breaking his nose for the second time. Myers fell to the floor, unconscious. Thomas kicked him in the ribs, still incensed at Myers' intention to use a broken bottle, recalling his own suffering from a similar weapon. He raised his foot once more, intending that Myers' face should be the target this time, but stopped when he saw the bottle and reached down for it. Thomas had no trouble smashing the bottle on the edge of the table and was left holding a jagged piece of glass.

'Jesus, he's going to do him with that bottle,' an onlooker shouted.

Thomas straddled the unconscious Myers and placed the jagged glass next to Myers' right eye, preparing to strake it across his face.

'He's going to take his eyes out. That kid's seen his last saloon-girl,' someone shouted. Maybe it was what the man had just said, or it might have been the sound of another, puking nearby, that caused Thomas to throw away the bottle, and let Myers keep his eyes, even though he didn't deserve to.

The burly barman asked one of the men to help him with Myers. He winked at Thomas as they carried Myers towards the door. One of the men from the card-game had spotted Myers' broken teeth on the floor.

'The next time he speaks he'll be whistling through that gap where his teeth used to be,' he quipped.

12

Just before sun-up Sheriff Brannigan headed his mount down Main Street and went on his way to take up position on the hillside half a mile from the town. He was confident that no one would have seen him leave and he was soon looking down from his vantage point at the trail below, hoping that he wouldn't have too long to wait before everything would be resolved. It would have been easier if Thomas had just left town as he'd planned a few days ago.

When Brannigan had first arrived in town he'd been tempted to introduce himself as a Shacklade. It wasn't as though he had reason to be ashamed of the name, but he doubted if he would have been asked to become sheriff if he had.

He'd been a scrawny kid when they had moved from Letana Creek following his brother Robert's murder. His own pa had been hanged just after he'd been born, but there had been no place for him in the Letana Creek graveyard, probably just a shallow grave near the tree that he'd swung from. He'd used the name Brannigan ever since his ma had remarried: a John Brannigan. According to his ma there had been three bullets lodged in his brother's back and she had always suspected that more than one person was involved. Brannigan had some very faint memories of the day that the sheriff brought the news, but he'd never forgotten seeing his ma crying every day for the next week or more. Sheriff Brewer had promised to catch the killer, but he never did, and that was why his ma decided to move on, hoping to put the memories behind her. Only a lengthy prison sentence for robbery had prevented him from returning to Letana Creek a long time ago.

★　★　★

Thomas was feeling edgy as he saddled the stallion, wondering what today would bring. He'd had further doubts during the night, remembering that he'd got it all wrong about Myers killing Ralph, but at least his late-night caller to the hotel had cleared up one thing.

He was aware of the risk he was taking and there was a chance that as soon as he rode down Main Street the killer would put a bullet in his back. Thomas put his foot in the stirrup and dismissed any thoughts of changing his mind. He'd made a plan and he would see it through, but his edginess heightened when he rode past the saloon, remembering his brief clash with Myers. The man lying near the steps of the saloon could be Myers, even though the clothes were different from what Myers had worn last night. He wondered if Myers had returned to the saloon, nursing his broken nose, looking for revenge. If he had, then he might have heard about Thomas's plans for this morning. Myers was a young man who would have pride, and he wouldn't have liked being beaten by an 'old man'. He would feel humiliated and that could be a powerful driving force for revenge. Thomas was preparing to dismount and check the condition of the man, when he heard the loud snoring. A closer look at the man revealed that it wasn't Myers, so Thomas heeled his mount forward, confident that it wasn't a trap.

He wished the sky wasn't so clear because it was going to be hot again later. That was another thing that the advancing years had brought him, a dislike of hot days. There was a time when he had crossed large stretches of desert pursuing a man and not felt the same discomfort he did now on a short trip in the heat. Perhaps he really was ready for long days in the shade on the banks of the river or a quiet spot on Main Street, watching the world go by like Matty and Jake, but all that was in the future, assuming he had a future.

He needed to concentrate on today.

Passing the cemetery he was reminded of Josh Stone and not Shacklade. Today was really all about Josh and a debt he hoped to repay him, not as well as he would have liked, but the next best thing. Thomas was no tracker, but he was certain that his stallion wasn't the first animal to kick up the dust on the trail this morning. He urged the stallion forward, eager to get things over with and he felt that familiar tension that came from the anticipation of action. The stallion would make sure that Thomas would be a difficult target as they moved at great speed. He wouldn't be looking over his shoulder for the rest of the journey, and he didn't expect he would need to ride all the way to the Brewer place. His experience told him that if anything was going to happen it would be close to Letana Creek.

He had ridden barely a mile from town when he approached the spot where he feared that someone might be waiting for him. When he drew level with the rocks he braced himself ready to react. He had already removed his rifle from its saddle scabbard and laid it across the saddle in case any shots might be fired outside the range of his pistol. The waiting for gunfire brought back memories of the occasions when he had been pursuing a wanted man, knowing that his quarry had a gun pointing at him from behind the cover of some trees or rocks. It was a fear like no other, waiting to feel the impact of a bullet fired off by an unseen foe.

He glanced from side to side while struggling to control the stallion as it became jumpy, sensing Thomas's fear or some hidden danger. When he was back into open ground Thomas expelled air from his lungs in a huge sigh of relief, but a sense of disappointment that perhaps his plan had failed. He was considering replacing the rifle back in its scabbard when the shot rang out, causing the stallion to rear up and the rifle to fall. Thomas was soon following his rifle to the ground after the second shot thudded into his shoulder He fell heavily and he didn't hear the third shot that shattered the quietness of the early morning.

$\star$ $\star$ $\star$

It was nearly dark when Jake Stookey and Matty Conlan made their way down Main Street, heading home to the tiny cabin that they shared.

'What do you think will happen to the marshal's fine horse and his belongings now that he's dead?' asked Matty.

'I expect someone will try and trace his family,' replied Jake. 'Anyway, he ain't dead yet.'

'Well he looked dead according to those who saw him being brought in this morning. He was a big feller and I expect Henry Mason will be charging extra for his box. I tell ya for nothin', I wouldn't want to be one of those carrying him.'

'I hope you're wrong about him

being dead, Matty. I kinda liked old one-eye, especially after he gave us that whiskey. I felt a bit guilty sending him to the Brewer place knowing that Brewer was lying there rotting where he'd died.'

'Who's Brewer?'

Jake gave a sigh.

'Brewer was the old town sheriff. Don't you remember Foggy Slater telling us about a year back, just before he died himself, that he'd called on Brewer and found him dead? Foggy reckoned the old bugger had probably died in his sleep just sitting in his chair. Perhaps we'll go the same way, but I'd sooner die outside the saloon.'

Matty was thinking that his old buddy was feeling a bit maudlin but there was no denying that such thoughts had crossed his mind as well.

'If we went together I wonder how long it would be before anyone noticed!'

Jake considered his friend's poser for a moment and then replied:

'When the saloon and the store noticed that they were selling less whiskey.'

★ ★ ★

Doc Shultz wiped the blood from his hands with a cloth that was already deeply reddened, picked up the whiskey-glass and slugged back the contents.

'I'm going to need more vhiskey,' he announced.

Brannigan was thinking that Shultz had consumed enough hard liquor, but it was probably the only thing that made his job bearable. The flies were beginning to gather on the body that had been laid in the corner waiting for Henry Mason to arrange its removal when he returned to town tomorrow morning. Brannigan offered to fetch the whiskey.

'The vhiskey isn't just for me,' said the doc. 'The bullet took a chunk out of a bone and ripped open a number of nerve ends.'

142

'Is he going to be all right, Doc?'

'He'll be fine, the wound is messy but it isn't serious,' the doc mused. 'But he took quite a bump on the head when he fell from his horse. If it hadn't been for you I suppose he would be the one heading for the undertaker's instead of him down there.'

Brannigan repeated his promise to return later with the whiskey, but first he had to call on someone and tell them bad news.

Brannigan returned to the surgery with the whiskey, and he discovered that the doc was asleep and Marshal Thomas looked dead to the world. He carefully placed the bottle on the table next to Shultz and tiptoed out of the room.

★ ★ ★

When Brannigan crossed the street the following morning he received some back-slapping and was feted like a hero. Jake Stookey and Matty Colgan were in their usual spot and Brannigan heard Matty's remark that was intended for Jake.

'Jesus, that lawman sure is sprightly for a man who was supposed to be dead last night. And he looks younger.'

The foul smell hit Brannigan's nostrils when he opened the surgery door. The loud snoring was coming from the doc who was slumped in the chair. The whiskey-bottle beside him was empty.

Brannigan crept towards Thomas to get a closer look but he could see that he hadn't changed his position since he'd seen him last night.

'I'm not dead, if that's what you're thinking,' Thomas growled, startling Brannigan. Before he could reply Thomas spoke again.

'Why didn't you plug that son of a bitch before he got a shot off?'

'Sorry about that, but we agreed that we had to be sure we'd got our man,' replied Brannigan.

'Well, come on then. Tell me who it

was,' ordered Thomas.

Brannigan looked puzzled.

'Don't you remember? I told you yesterday before I brought you here,' he replied. 'That's his body in the corner there, waiting for Henry Mason to pick it up. It was Jeff Lowrie.'

'Well I'll be damned,' said Thomas. 'I had him down as a sneak but not a killer. But it fits in with what we discussed when you called at my hotel.'

When Brannigan had visited Thomas at his hotel he told him that he'd worked out that he was trying to bring the killer out into the open when Joe Dalton mentioned to him that Thomas had broadcast his intentions in the saloon. Brannigan had revealed that he was Robert Shacklade's brother but had sworn that he'd had nothing to do with the killings. He'd offered to prove that he wasn't even in town on the day that the first killing took place.

'I guess I have a lot to thank you and the doc for, Brannigan. I never would have guessed you were Robert Shacklade's brother and the man responsible for placing the flowers on his grave. So how does it feel, knowing that your brother's death has probably been avenged after all this time?'

'To be honest, Marshal, I feel pretty bad about the whole thing. I hardly knew my brother, but as I explained to you, I promised my ma that I would lay flowers on his grave if ever I came this way. Now I'm feeling that I might have caused the death of some innocent men even though it was unintentional.'

'Have you told Lowrie's wife what happened? Perhaps she could shed some light on things.'

Brannigan nodded.

'She took it pretty badly,' he said, 'but she couldn't help much, except to say that he'd taken to wearing a gun on occasions. Apparently Lowrie's excuse for being on the trail so early on the morning he came after you was that he was going to see someone in Jolin Town to organize supplies for the store. She's

Lowrie's second wife and they haven't been married long. I still don't understand why Lowrie would have felt threatened by what happened to my brother, especially after all this time.'

Thomas eased himself up.

'My guess would be that all the men who died, apart from Cutler, knew something about what happened to your brother,' he replied. 'When you started placing flowers on the grave it stirred up old memories. If Lowrie was the one who killed your brother he wouldn't have wanted to have his political ambitions messed up if anyone revealed that he was a killer. Why else would he have come after me unless he thought old Brewer was alive and really did know something about it?'

Brannigan sighed.

'I guess what you say sort of fits together,' he said, not totally convinced.

As soon as Brannigan left, Doc Shultz reached for the whiskey-bottle. He cursed when he discovered it was empty.

'I take it that you haven't met Mary Lowrie?' Shultz enquired, indicating that he had been listening to Brannigan's and Thomas's conversation.

'As a matter of fact, I haven't,' replied Thomas, puzzled by the tone of Shultz's question.

'She's not the sort of woman that a man would ever forget, nor would he leave her bed at an ungodly hour unless he had some very important business to attend to.'

'Brannigan said they hadn't been married long. Is she a local woman?'

'No, she's a Texas girl. Some folks say that she was a mail-order bride, but Lowrie was always a bit coy as to how they met. Their marriage caused quite a stir at the time, what with his first wife being buried only three months earlier, and Mary being almost young enough to be his granddaughter. Now she's a very rich young woman. I've heard talk that she and Sheriff Brannigan are very close.'

Thomas wasn't really interested in

the gossip about Mary Lowrie and he was soon settling back down for another sleep.

Thomas was strong enough to leave Letana Creek within a week of some folks diagnosing his premature death. The doc warned him about the head injury and told him not to be surprised if he started having headaches or he discovered that his memory wasn't as good as it used to be.

Thomas had paid a visit to Barbara and Shelley Stone the night before to say another farewell. He had expected to leave unnoticed, but a small crowd had gathered near the hotel to see him off. He didn't speak to any of them, but gave a polite nod as he mounted the stallion. Jake and Matty were in their usual seats across the street and he waved to them before he turned the animal, then heeled it to start his journey home.

'That one-eyed feller is dumber than he looks, wearing a gun belt with his arm in a sling,' Matty said when Thomas was out of earshot.

The journey was always going to bring back memories of the events of a week ago and what led up to them. He hadn't worked things out too well, suspecting the wrong people, but at least it had all ended satisfactorily. He hoped that his messages and letter had reached Olive because otherwise she was probably thinking he was dead by now.

He was still thinking of Olive when he reached the group of rocks where Lowrie had tried to kill him. Thomas was thinking that he'd had enough of killing. He was going home to live in peace. He'd done more killing than any one else he knew, but it would end here. Thomas removed his holster, then fondly caressed the Peacemaker Colt before he placed it in the holster. He hurled the holster and weapon as far as he could. He heard them land amongst the small rocks and hoped the gun would never be found and used again, perhaps to end another life.

13

It felt like old times as he headed down Statton Crossing's Main Street. He was coming home after a successful mission, but this would be the last time. There might be another call for help, but he would never leave Statton Crossing again without Olive by his side. Luck had been with him these past weeks, but he hadn't needed luck when he was younger, and he wouldn't be relying on it again.

Thomas nudged the stallion towards Cawley's store and pulled it up outside, satisfied that it seemed he had won the battle of wills with his horse.

Merle Cawley had been a deputy in the town until he had to have an arm amputated after being shot at close range by a bank-robber. He had known Thomas a long time and always looked forward to their chinwags.

'Welcome back, Marshal. You must have an understanding wife. My Tilly wouldn't let me have a day at the rodeo, let alone a lengthy fishing-trip like you've just had. You don't exactly look kitted-up for fishing, though.'

'That's because I haven't been fishing, Merle. I've been away sorting out a bit of trouble for a very old friend.'

Cawley noticed that Thomas wasn't armed, and he wondered what sort of trouble the marshal had sorted out. It reminded him that he had some news to tell.

'Sheriff Vogel was out of town last night and we could have done with your help when the Molloys tried to cause trouble.'

'Denny and Joey are usually harmless. A few shots in the air isn't worth getting upset about,' commented Thomas casually.

'It wasn't Denny and Joey who caused the trouble.' Cawley paused and then continued: 'Of course, you wouldn't know about Zak and Lee getting out of prison last week. They came in here and threatened to burn the store down unless I sold them some ammunition. I don't think they've been sober since they got back. Zak was asking about you, Marshal.'

Thomas didn't know how the two oldest Molloy brothers had got out of prison, but even they wouldn't have been stupid enough to head home if they'd escaped.

'What did Zak Molloy have to say for himself?' Thomas asked, concerned that the brothers might be planning something.

'He said that he hoped that you weren't dead and was looking forward to meeting you again. He had that sickly sneer on his face at the time. It doesn't look as though life in prison has taught them a lesson. Anyway, what can I get you, Marshal?'

Thomas cleared his throat.

'Hmm, I'm not one for shopping, Merle, as you know, but I'm looking for a present for Olive, a piece of jewellery.

Do you sell that sort of thing?'

Merle smiled at the thought of Thomas doing anything romantic.

'It just so happens that I had a selection of brooches arrive a couple of days ago.'

The storekeeper reached below the counter and placed the tray of brooches in front of Thomas. Within seconds he'd chosen the one with a small green emerald set in a gold leaf.

'I'll take that one,' he said, eager to get the purchase over with.

'You've got taste, Marshal, but although it's the smallest piece on the tray, it's also the most expensive at fifteen dollars.'

'Just make sure that you put it in a nice box,' Thomas ordered, still feeling uncomfortable about making the purchase.

'You wouldn't be in some sort of trouble with Olive would you, Marshal?'

Thomas's glower was enough to make the storekeeper get on with placing the brooch in a box. While he did, Thomas was thinking of the Molloy brothers whom he had helped send to prison.

'You'd better show me whatever pistols you've got, Merle, as well as a decent holster, and I'll have a box of shells.'

Thomas spent much longer over choosing his pistol than he had over the brooch. Eventually he had got the choice down to two when Merle tried to influence him.

'I'll tell you what, Marshal; I'll let you have one of those pearl-handled specials for the same price as the Peacemakers that you're deliberating over. Try it and see how it feels. It would be a bargain at the price I'm offering it to you.'

Thomas accepted the invitation and picked up the weapon, but he was soon offering it back to Merle.

'I wouldn't have that gun if you gave it me for free. The balance is all wrong. A man could get himself killed if he was relying on that weapon.' Thomas picked up one of the two he had been agonizing over. 'I'll take this one,' he said.

Merle looked disappointed at not being able to get rid of the fancy weapon even at a knock-down price. He offered to wrap up the marshal's choice, but wished he hadn't.

'It won't be much use to me wrapped up if the Molloys start shooting at me when I step back out on to Main Street,' Thomas growled as he started buckling on the belt and holster. He'd discarded the sling on the outskirts of town, not wishing to alarm Olive.

Thomas headed the stallion up Main Street after concluding his business at the store, quietly cursing the Molloys. He was also regretting that he had cleared all his old pistols out of the house when he'd married Olive and that he'd thrown his favourite gun away amongst the rocks near Letana Creek.

As he drew closer to his home on the far side of town it revived memories of his first marriage when he had returned after being involved in something dangerous, knowing that his wife had been left worrying and wondering if he was still alive.

He would normally stable his horse at the livery first, but today he decided to head straight home. It was the first time he had been parted from Olive, and he smiled thinking about the treats he would be in for, including her special beef and potatoes, a glass of beer and apple-pie. His anticipation was dulled when he realized that she might not even be at home. She was often out trying to help someone or other.

Thomas was tying the stallion to the white fence at the front of his house when he saw the figure approaching.

'Jesus,' he said under his breath.

The Reverend Silas Boscombe was a nice enough man, but Thomas was anxious to see Olive and didn't want to get involved in a lengthy chinwag.

Thomas was staring at the holes in his front door when Silas Boscombe told him that Olive wasn't at home.

There was no mistaking that someone had shot up the front door. He turned to the Reverend Boscombe, a man who usually carried too many worries on his thin face. Today he looked as though he had collected a few more.

'I'm afraid there was some trouble here last night, Marshal, while Mrs Thomas was inside the house.' Thomas felt the same sense of desperation as when the doctor had told him that his first wife wouldn't last the night. He had gone outside and looked up to the night sky, while he begged a God he didn't believe in, to spare her. He'd pleaded with God to take him in her place.

'Marshal, I said your wife is safe and staying with us,' the Reverend Boscombe repeated. Thomas came out of his trance. He hadn't begged God this time, but he would have done.

'I'd better go and bring her home,' said a relieved but angry Thomas. 'She'd better not have suffered any harm,' he added, his threat directed at the Molloy brothers, even though he didn't know if they'd been responsible for the holes in his front door.

'Mrs Thomas is fine,' replied the minister. 'She's more worried about you than herself.'

Later that night as Thomas cradled Olive in his arms he was thinking of how he'd felt when he had been separated from her, and how devastated he'd been when he thought he'd lost her earlier that day. There were things he needed to say to her before it was too late.

'Olive, you know I'm not much good at sweet-talking, never have been.'

He couldn't see Olive smile in the dim light of the bedroom, but he felt her squeeze his hand.

'Oh, I think you'll manage all right when you want to disappear for a day's fishing,' she teased.

'You also know that I'm never ever going to forget my Mary. She was special to me, but so are you. I love you in a way that is no different from what my love for Mary was. I'm a lucky man to have you, and I want to grow really old with you.'

She leaned over and kissed him on the cheek and he felt the warm tears on her face.

'And that's what I want, Ned. Does that mean that you won't be leaving me again to help someone, putting what we have at risk?'

Thomas knew that there was no easy way to explain what he had to do, and he hoped that she would understand.

'I've never gone looking for trouble, Olive, but it has often found me, just like now with the Molloy brothers. I know how their minds work and they'll be back, maybe not for a week or a month, but they'll come after me, as sure as night follows day.'

Olive had described the two men she had seen from the window just before the shooting had started. Thomas had told her that the description fitted the brothers.

She knew now that Thomas wouldn't put their future at risk unless he felt that he had no real choice, but she was frightened and suggested an alternative.

'But we could leave. We have enough put by to start a new home. We could find somewhere safe and quiet where they'd never find us.'

Thomas cuddled her again and sighed, wishing that he could agree with her, but he couldn't.

'It wouldn't work, honey. I'm not going to run away, and it's not because of stupid pride. I'm too long in the tooth to worry about my reputation. It's because they would find us, and even if they didn't, we would spend the rest of our lives waiting and watching for them.'

'There must be something that can be done,' she pleaded, her voice sounding desperate. 'Surely Sheriff Vogel can arrest them for what they did here. They could have killed me.'

'Young Vogel's a fine sheriff, and he isn't frightened of the Molloys. I spoke to him this afternoon when I took my horse to the livery and we discussed the brothers. We've worked out a plan that might just provide a solution without anyone getting hurt.'

Thomas explained to her that he and Vogel were going out to the Molloy place tomorrow. They would tell the brothers that if they called off their vendetta against Thomas they wouldn't be arrested for shooting up the house. Their pa, Sheb Molloy, was a reasonable man, and he could help by making Zak and Lee see sense. It might save them from going back to prison or ending up with a noose around their neck.

'But that's silly. You'll be going into the lion's den and from what you said earlier they don't sound like the sort of men who would listen to reason.'

'Honey, I won't be in any danger. The Molloys are too cowardly for a face-to-face confrontation. That's not their style, otherwise they would have waited and approached me rather than hope they would get lucky by firing through the door like they did. I'm not going to be in any danger and it might just work. Anyway, Vogel will be with me. He's young and handy with his gun. A bit too fancy for my liking, with all that twirling stuff, but he's good and he's on my side. Now let's get some sleep. It's been a long day for both of us. And you remember what I said about you, and our future. I'm not going to risk losing that.'

★   ★   ★

Olive had hardly managed to sleep at all and was awake when Thomas eased himself out of the bed, hoping that he wouldn't disturb her. By the time he'd washed and dressed, his breakfast of eggs and beans was waiting for him. They ate in silence, but despite an atmosphere of anxiety there was also a closeness that had come from their declarations to each other the previous night.

It would be another two hours before he headed off to the Molloys. He was wishing that he had gone yesterday afternoon without telling Olive, so saving her from the anguish she was feeling now. He told her about the trip to Letana Creek and Josh's death without mentioning the gory details. He didn't mention his own injuries, or what had happened to Ralph, and he was glad that she hadn't questioned him further.

He was relieved when it was time to buckle on his newly purchased gun belt, and prepare to leave. Olive followed him to the door, determined once again that she wouldn't cry and make things more difficult for him. He broke away from their embrace and held her at arm's length.

'I should be back in a couple of hours, but if I'm not, don't you go thinking that something's gone wrong. Remember, you don't get to my age in the business I was in unless you have a guardian angel or Lady Luck on your side. Well, I think I've got both. Now you make sure that you're not out visiting when I get back.' Thomas kissed her again, then made his way out through the bullet-riddled door and headed for the livery without looking back.

Sheriff Vogel was waiting for him outside his office, already mounted on his distinctive red roan. Brad Vogel had been sheriff for just over a year. He was twenty-five years old and built like the proverbial ox. The piercing blue eyes caused most villains and troublemakers to drop their eyelids. Thomas had no doubt that he would be a fine lawman one day. He had all the attributes and just needed the experience.

Vogel hadn't been keen on Thomas's idea of giving the Molloys a way out, but he had a lot of respect for Thomas and decided to go along with it. He only intended to give the Molloys this one chance; if they turned it down or messed up again he would throw them both in jail. Statton Crossing had been a peaceful town long before he took over and he intended to keep it that way.

The Molloy homestead was two miles west of the town and it wasn't long before Vogel and Thomas pulled up near the broken-down gate at the entrance. There didn't seem much use for the gate seeing that fencing either side had long since fallen down due to neglect.

Vogel sighed as they approached the tiny house.

'I expect this place has seen better times,' he said, trying to put it politely as he surveyed the obvious signs of neglect and squalor.

'Not since Myra Molloy died about two and bit years ago,' said Thomas. 'There's eleven children when they're all at home, but most are too young to do the heavy work, and the older ones are too idle.'

Vogel was used to seeing some of the kids rummaging through the bins near the store, but he'd never seen Sheb Molloy.

'Eleven children?' said Vogel and shook his head.

'And I expect poor Myra lost a few as well,' added Thomas.

Vogel had spotted the figure who had just stepped off the porch of the house, which looked as though it wouldn't survive the next serious storm.

'If that's Sheb Molloy, then he ain't come out to welcome us, seeing as how he's pointing a rifle in our direction,' Vogel remarked without any trace of alarm in his voice.

'That's Sheb,' Thomas confirmed. 'His eyesight's never been too good, so I doubt if he'd hit either of us from this range, even if he wanted to. Morning, Sheb,' he shouted out, causing Sheb to squint as they got nearer to him.

Sheb lowered his rifle before greeting Thomas. He apologized about the gun and then added:

'I thought it was those two varmints of mine coming back. I mean the two that they should have kept in jail.'

Thomas was thinking that they'd had

a wasted journey and was wondering why Sheb would want to point a rifle at his own sons.

'You look a bit troubled, Sheb. What's happened?' Thomas asked.

'There's been a bit of an upset here this morning, but you don't want to hear about my troubles. You'd better come inside and have a drink and tell me what brings you here. I guess the young feller must be Sheriff Vogel.'

Vogel smiled and simply said: 'Howdy, Mr Molloy.'

Sheb Molloy was forty-five years old, but he shuffled more than walked and could have passed for someone much older except for his full head of black curly hair. He coughed as he climbed the steps of the porch. The rattle from his chest only stopped when he cleared his throat and spat the green phlegm into the dust at the bottom of the steps.

'That mining job has a lot to answer for, I can tell ya, Marshal. It wasn't human working underground like that and now I cough my guts up every day.'

Rumour had it that Sheb had never seen the inside of a mine in his life, that his health problems were the legacy of too much rotgut whiskey and the fact that he was rarely seen without a cigarette or small cigar hanging from his lips.

The inside of the cabin was clean, and the children were spotless. Sheb clapped his hands and ordered the three girls and their brother to go about their chores outside.

There was a chorus of 'Yes, Pa', and Sheb shouted after them: 'Isobel, tell Billy to keep a look-out for his no good brothers and to let me know if Lee and Zak come back.'

'You must be proud of the little ones, Sheb, but I guess it must be hard at times,' said a bemused Thomas after he'd watched the youngsters scurry away.

'It's not easy, Marshal, but they're happy kids and that's all that matters. A young couple called by last week and wanted to adopt one of the twins. They would have given her a fine home and lots of loving. It would have been one less mouth to feed, but as long as I'm able they'll all stay together. Now what brings you out here, as if I didn't know? Well, you're too late. I ordered them out of here less than fifteen minutes ago, but I'd rather not say why. Family business, it was.'

Sheb poured them some whiskey from a strange-looking jar. Vogel had a good idea what its original use had been and declined the offering, but Thomas accepted the drink and was soon feeling that a small fire had started at the back of his throat.

'It's a wonder we didn't see the boys on the way here if they were headed for town,' Thomas said, thinking that he would finish his drink and leave.

'They headed for town all right, but you wouldn't see them unless you took a short cut across Nolan's land, because that's the way the boys would have gone,' Sheb explained.

'Whatever they did must have been

serious, Sheb, for you to send kin packing,' Thomas said, without intending to pry into family business.

'Damn, why should I bother shielding them?' Sheb growled. 'Zak was lusting after his own sister, Mary Lou. Tried forcing himself on her and would have done, if Billy hadn't stopped him. Then Lee and Zak turned on Billy. One of the little ones came running for me and I told them to go and never to come back. Lee ain't as evil as his brother, but I came within a whisker of shooting them both.'

Thomas shook his head, but he wasn't shocked. No one who had met the brothers would have been. They were capable of anything, and if it hadn't been for some fool of a judge they should have swung from a rope or rotted in jail. They didn't belong amongst normal civilized folk.

Thomas felt a sense of alarm and was eager to get back to town and Olive.

'We'd best be off, then, Sheb. There's no point in discussing why we came calling. Thanks for the drink.'

When Thomas and Vogel reached the door, Sheb called after them.

'Marshal, you ought to know that Zak's been saying that they have some unfinished business with you and your wife. Just before they left Zak said that your wife would give him what he couldn't get from their sister, if you know what I mean. Her age won't matter none to them, but I guess you already know that.'

Thomas didn't reply as he headed for his horse at a speed that belied his age and the state of his gammy leg. He was mounted before Vogel, and the chickens scattered as he urged the stallion forward. He hadn't heard Sheb Molloy shout out:

'If you kill 'em don't bother telling me,' and adding in a lowered voice: 'They won't be mourned by anyone here.'

Thomas had pushed the stallion, and when he steered it through the gate and on to Nolan land, the pursuing Vogel was nowhere in sight. The stallion had a big heart and Thomas urged it on like never before. When he reached the town the horse was blowing hard. Thomas didn't ease up as he rode down Main Street, and he was disappointed to see that there was only one horse tied to the rail outside the saloon. He had been hoping that the Molloys might have stopped off at the saloon before going about their evil work.

The sight of the small group of people and Doc Jones's carriage outside his house, made Thomas groan with despair. The anguished faces were lowered as he ran up the path towards the door, brushing aside the Reverend Boscombe who had just come out of the house. The warning words that he would 'have to be brave' had not registered with Thomas.

There was no anger in him, only increased despair when he saw Olive lying on the floor, her face showing a pale expression that grieved and frightened him. There was a large purple bruise on the side of her face, but the calico dress was, as always, spotless. Then he saw the redness and bruising on her throat. Doc Jones was kneeling beside her and turned to face Thomas. The doctor shook his head before Thomas had the chance to ask how she was.

'She's hanging on, Marshal, but she's gotten worse since I arrived and gone into some kind of coma. I was about to ask someone to help me move her to the bed, but I expect you'll want to do that now.'

'But can't you save her, Doc? You must be able to do something,' Thomas pleaded desperately.

'Let's make her comfortable, Marshal, and then we can talk,' was all the doctor replied, unable to provide any words of comfort without lying to Thomas.

Thomas lifted up his beloved Olive and carried her to the bed where he had held her so intimately just a short time ago. Doc Jones stayed in the main room to give Thomas a chance to have a private moment with his wife. If he hadn't he might have seen something never witnessed by another human being: tears on Thomas's face. It was the faint smile that she had given him just before she had drifted off into unconsciousness again that had got to him. He gently brushed her hair to the side and covered her lower body with the bed sheet before leaving.

'She recognized me, Doc, surely there must be some hope?' he pleaded once again.

'It's times like this that we medical folk feel so inadequate, Marshal. Someone tried to strangle her and she must have taken a heavy fall or been struck a massive blow to the head. There's nothing I can do for her. It's not as though she's got a wound that can be treated. If she did recognize you then it means that her brain may not have been damaged, but there's a chance that she didn't actually see you even though she smiled. She's in God's hands now and I fear that we'll need a miracle.'

Thomas felt the anger rise in him. He wanted revenge against whoever might have destroyed the new life he had planned with Olive. He asked the question that he believed he already knew the answer to, and that was who had been responsible.

'I don't know who did this terrible thing, Marshal,' Doc Jones replied. 'Olive was found by the Reverend's wife when she called in. When I got here, Olive was drifting in and out of consciousness and I couldn't make out most of what she said, except that it sounded as though two men were looking for you.'

Thomas didn't want to ask, but he needed to know the answer to another nagging question.

'Doc, whoever did this to Olive, did they molest her in any way? I've got my reasons for asking this.'

'I had to disturb her clothes to see if there were any more injuries, Marshal,

176

but there was no sign of what you're asking, none at all.'

'You wouldn't lie to make me feel better, because you'd be covering up for scum.'

'I'm telling you the truth, Marshal. It looks like whoever it was might have panicked. You can see from the overturned furniture that Olive must have put up a fierce struggle and I wouldn't be surprised if whoever attacked her was carrying an injury of some kind. There were traces of blood under Olive's fingernails, indicating that she had scratched at least one of her attackers.'

Thomas was relieved that Olive hadn't been violated. At least she'd been spared that, but it didn't lessen the anger he felt towards the Molloys. He was startled when Vogel placed a comforting hand on his shoulder.

'Vogel, those bastards have hurt my Olive. I should have let you arrest them like you wanted. If she dies it will be my fault.'

'I'll get a posse together, Marshal. They must have headed towards Nashmora because they would have run into one of us at some point if they had gone west out of town. I came back on the main trail and you must have cut across the Nolan land so one of us would have seen them.'

'No,' Thomas roared. 'No posse. I'm going to sit with my Olive for a little while and pray. Then I'm going after the Molloys, on my own.'

Vogel didn't want to add to Thomas's upset.

'If that's what you want, Marshal, then I'll go along with it. I know you're feeling raw at the moment, but those two aren't worth hanging for. They'll get what they deserve if you let the law take care of them.'

Vogel had said what he had to, but he didn't expect it to have any effect on Thomas. Short of locking him up, nothing could be done to stop Thomas doing it his way. The point was reinforced when Thomas said:

'They'll get what they deserve,' and stifled any further discussion by adding, 'Now, I'm going to sit with my wife.'

By the time sunlight came through the tiny window, Thomas had barely snatched a few minutes' sleep in the chair beside the bed while he had waited for signs that Olive might regain consciousness. She had groaned quietly, causing his hopes to be raised, but she had never opened her eyes, not even as he bathed her face with a soft cloth.

Thomas felt guilty when he left her side in order to wash himself and change his clothes. Then he ate for the first time since Olive had made his breakfast close to twenty-four hours earlier, knowing that he would need all his strength later.

Doc Jones was the first caller and hid his surprise that Olive was still alive.

'She's a battler, Marshal, but you shouldn't get your hopes up. Did you manage to get her to take any water?'

Thomas shook his head and Doc Jones sighed.

'It's important she takes some liquid, but at least she doesn't seem any worse than last night and that's good news. Why don't you try and get some sleep, Marshal, while I sit with her.'

Before Thomas could tell the doc that he had things to do, Mrs Boscombe arrived. She was distressed to hear that Olive's condition had not improved. She had brought a basket of items, including a book which she told Thomas was one that Olive was looking forward to reading.

'I thought that I might sit and read some of it to her,' she added, her eyes glistening. Mrs Boscombe then asked him if he had decided what to do about going after whoever had done this terrible thing to Olive.

'It hasn't been easy, Mrs Boscombe, and some folks might think badly of me leaving her at a time like this, but if you are prepared to stay with her, and make sure that she's never left on her own, then I'll be on my way once you've settled in.'

Mrs Boscombe couldn't abide violence and didn't agree with the preaching of an eye for eye, but she was more tactful than her husband, and she wasn't about to start explaining the virtues of forgiveness to the marshal.

The doctor had heard Thomas's plans but didn't comment on them. Before he left he promised to make regular visits until Thomas returned.

As Thomas prepared to leave, he asked Mrs Boscombe to give him just a few minutes alone with his wife. He sat on the edge of the bed and held Olive's tiny hand. He gave it a gentle squeeze.

'I've got to do this honey; I think you will know that. I couldn't live with myself if I didn't. Once it's over I'll be back as quick as that big horse of mine can get me here, and God willing you'll be sitting up and out of danger. Don't you let me down now, do you hear me?' Thomas paused after his mock bullying and leaned forward. 'You're a special lady, Olive Thomas, and I love you.'

Ten minutes later Thomas was at the

livery and saddling his horse. He ignored the pain in his shoulder as he performed the routine that he'd done so often, preparing to hunt someone down. It was different this time because he was no longer a lawman, and it was personal. He would be in Nashmora within an hour and if the Molloys were there he would discover whether he had faith in the law, and what sort of man he really was.

14

Zak Molloy felt the dig in his ribs, but he had trouble opening his eyes to see who had delivered it. He didn't recognize the voice that said:

'Come on, lover boy. Your time's up unless you want to hand over some more money.'

His eyes eventually opened and he saw Melissa, the woman giving the orders. He was racking his brains to try and remember how he could have ended up in bed with this flabby woman — she was old enough to be his ma. He grimaced as he watched her apply the thick lipstick and a generous helping of face powder, using a finger to try and fill the wrinkles around the eyes with the powder. She was holding the handmirror close to her face, studying the puffiness beneath the eyes, using a finger in an attempt to disperse the bags. She only succeeded in leaving a reddened ridge which was stark against the white powder.

'I would've let you sleep longer, honey, but I have strict house rules. By the way, considering how much hard liquor you downed last night you got your money's worth. I thought I was in for a good night's sleep, but I'm not complaining.'

Zak rubbed his eyes and studied the grotesque creature he now recognized as the woman in charge of the saloon girls. He had paid Colette, the leggy blonde beauty, and couldn't understand how come he'd ended up with Madame Horror. He swung his legs to get out of bed and saw the naked figure of a man lying on the floor.

'Jesus, what the shit's a dead man doing on the floor,' Zak gasped.

Melissa took a long drag on the cigarette that she had just loaded into the pearl cigarette-holder before she answered.

'That's your brother, and he wasn't

dead half an hour ago when he was getting his money's worth out of me as well. You sure are a horny pair.'

Zak took a closer look at the man who was now snoring loudly, then picked up the jug of water and poured it over his brother's naked body. Lee Molloy was awakened with a shock, which was followed by another when he set eyes on Melissa.

'Where's Cloe?' he asked, remembering handing over his money to the busty brunette, after he'd pushed away a dude who had also planned to bed her.

'Colette and Cloe were very popular girls last night,' Melissa explained, 'and they couldn't fit you boys in. I had you both carried up here and you drifted off to sleep. I knew how horny you both were and how disappointed you'd be missing out on what you came for, so I crept in beside you and let you take turns with me.'

'How do we know that we got what we paid for, 'cos I don't remember anything and I want my money back,'

Lee said, suspecting that the old bitch was telling them a pack of lies.

'Listen, sonny, you both got your money's worth. I normally charge extra for a threesome, but made an exception with you being brothers. The house rule is that no one ever gets their money back and walks out of here. Why don't you get dressed, freshen yourselves up and go get some breakfast. You both look like shit.'

Melissa headed for the door as the brothers started to dress. Neither of them fancied tackling her barmen George and Henry who would be downstairs. At least not at the moment.

Ten minutes later the brothers were wolfing down their breakfast in the diner opposite the saloon. Lee had been born twenty-three years ago, just eleven months after Zak. Lee had inherited the thick, black, curly hair of his pa while Zak's hair was straight and closer to being ginger than fair. Apart from the hair-colouring the brothers could have passed as twins.

Both were broad-shouldered and narrow-hipped, pug-nosed with bushy eyebrows and with a full set of straight tobacco-stained teeth.

'What are we going to do now, Zak? Do you think Marshal Thomas will come after us because of what we did?'

Zak wiped the grease from his chin with the back of his hand.

'Of course he won't. I bet it's not the first time that someone fired a few shots at his house. We knew he wasn't at home, so we didn't do any real harm. Anyway, you're forgetting that Thomas ain't the same dude who sent us to prison. He's old and he's all washed up according to what we've been told. Now Vogel's a different matter. I wouldn't fancy taking him on even if there are two of us.'

Lee paused from shovelling beans into his mouth.

'I still ain't happy about that old bitch Melissa tricking us the way she did.'

'Don't worry, we'll get even with her,

and leave here with more money than we came with. Talking of money, how much have you got left?'

Lee fished into his pockets and placed the crumpled dollar notes on the table.

'Never mind counting, there's enough there,' Zak snapped. 'Let's go and pay ugly Melissa another visit. And leave the talking to me.'

* * *

Melissa had just lit her seventh cigarette of the morning as she sat at the bar, where Zak and Lee approached her. She took a deep sigh.

'Now I hope you boys don't plan on making trouble because Henry and George will oblige you if that's what you want.'

Zak smiled showing the traces of bean and egg between his teeth. 'We ain't come for trouble, we're here for business, honey.'

Melissa looked up at the clock on the

wall behind the bar.

'Then you're about ten hours too early if you want Cloe and Colette, because they don't start work until then.'

Zak grinned and looked Melissa up and down before his eyes stayed locked on her cleavage.

'We ain't interested in those girls, not any more. We want another session with you, now that we're properly sobered up. That's if it's the same price as last night.'

Melissa smiled.

'I'd be delighted boys, but Henry will be disappointed because I was just telling him that I was feeling up for it and had offered him a free one. If you'd come ten minutes later, Henry would have finished cleaning those glasses and followed me upstairs.' Melissa smiled at Henry and then apologized for the change of plan.

'Sorry, Henry, honey, you'll have to wait until later. You know business always comes first.' Melissa turned towards the brothers, 'Now, boys, let's have your money, and then we can make ourselves comfortable upstairs.'

When the money was handed over, the threesome made their way upstairs, leaving behind a relieved Henry, who was about to become the butt of George's tormenting.

The bedroom looked just the same as when they had left it earlier in the morning, except that the pot in the corner had been emptied and the air was a bit sweeter. Melissa wasted no time in removing her garments, while the brothers stood and watched. The sight of Melissa'a flesh had Zak deciding to delay gagging the old bitch and stealing her money. Zak fumbled as he started unbuckling his belt, leaving his brother somewhat confused. 'You ain't really going to do it with her now, Zak?' asked Lee, shocked that his brother would consider it in the cold light of day.

'Are you dumb? Of course I'm going to do it with her,' replied Zak, his voice thick with the effect of his rising passion, as he struggled to unbuckle his belt. 'She's a real woman, can't you see that! You'd better get ready because I don't think I'm going to be long.'

Zak was thinking that she might not be pretty, but she could make up for that with her experience. He had a special liking for older women and he could tell that she was just as ready as he was.

Melissa was flushed with her own excitement at the way the young feller had just paid her a compliment. He wanted her real bad and he was cold sober. She would make sure that he wasn't disappointed as she lay back on the bed and raised her arms inviting him towards her. But she was inter-upted when Lee muttered something about not staying around to watch and left.

Zak eventually got the stubborn buckle undone and had lowered his pants when Melissa heard the door handle turn. She hoped the brother with the black curly hair had changed his mind because he was cute, but the man who entered the room wasn't young and he was pointing a gun at the brother whose passion was already obvious. Zak Molloy was about to turn and see what Melissa was looking at when the bullet hit him in the back of the head.

Melissa had seen some gruesome sights in bar-room brawls, mostly from broken bottles being thrust into faces, and she wasn't the screaming kind, especially when a gun was being pointed at her. The old feller holding the gun signalled for her to be quiet and then ordered her to get up and shout downstairs to the bartenders that everything was OK. He made it clear that if she didn't she would be joining her dead customer.

Melissa's voice was calm as she shouted downstairs that the shot had been fired by accident and that everything was fine. Henry was half-way up the stairs, but retreated after hearing her call out.

She didn't know how the killer had got up to the room without being seen, but it must have been through the bar because now he was asking her if there was a back way out of the saloon. She wasn't sure if he would manage the rear exit, but she offered to show him the way if he waited while she got dressed. She didn't argue when he told her there wasn't time for dressing and she led him in her naked state along the corridor to a room which had steps on the outside.

'Why did you kill that young feller,' she asked after she had shown him the way he could escape.

'Because he deserved it,' he replied without any show of emotion.

Melissa was wondering where the other brother was but it looked as though he'd had a lucky escape.

15

It was approaching mid day when Vogel tied the reins of his mount to the rail outside the sheriff's office in Nashmora. He had only met Sheriff Adley once, but he was certain that he would assist him in arresting the Molloy brothers if they were in town. Thomas would be annoyed when he found out that he had gone looking for the brothers after being warned off, but Vogel would risk upsetting Thomas if it meant saving him from a hanging. Apart from his concern for Marshal Thomas, Vogel wasn't totally convinced that either of the Molloy brothers had attacked Olive Thomas. If he could arrest the Molloys before Thomas got to them, he could put them in jail awaiting trial and that would be best for everyone, especially Thomas.

'If you're looking for the sheriff he

ain't here,' was the greeting Vogel got from the slovenly-looking deputy who carried on eating the giant size chunks of bread and cheese.

'When will he be back?' Vogel asked.

'Shouldn't be too long, he's down at the undertaker's. This used to be a quiet town, but not any more. Two killings before noon is enough to put a man off his grub.'

Vogel was already thinking the worst when he asked what had happened.

'I don't rightly know all the details because the sheriff hurried away, telling me to hold the fort, so to speak, because two people had been killed over at the saloon. My hunch would be that there was some argument over one of the saloon girls.'

Vogel was about to ask a question when Sheriff Adley came in, looking anxious, but he smiled when he saw Vogel.

'Good to see you again, Vogel. I was talking to old Marshal Thomas not more than half an hour ago, but he didn't mention that you were in town as well. We've had two killings here this morning. You'll know one of them, goes by the name of Zak Molloy from your neck of the woods.'

Vogel groaned inwardly as he realized that he'd arrived too late to save Thomas. He had hoped that he would have stayed with his wife, but it looked as though sweet Olive must have died.

Vogel told Sheriff Adley that he was making a social call and was hoping to have a chinwag. He lied when he said that he didn't know why Thomas had been in town. Then he asked what Thomas had said.

'Not a lot really, but he sure as hell saved me a lot of trouble when he identified Zak Molloy. He thinks his brother Lee killed him. He doesn't change much and he sure seemed in a hurry to get back home.'

Vogel was in a quandary as to whether he should tell Adley that he'd really come to Nashmora to stop Thomas from killing the brothers.

'So who was the other man who died?' asked Vogel.

'It wasn't a man. It was Melissa, the woman who runs the brothel connected to the saloon. It appears that she'd gone upstairs to entertain Zak and his brother, but there was no sign of Lee Molloy. Zak had his pants around his ankles when he died from a single shot and Melissa had been strangled. The brother must have stolen Melissa's money because none was found and Melissa wouldn't have been entertaining them for free. Damn, I should have mentioned to Thomas about a witness seeing the killer, but the description of the suspect didn't fit Lee Molloy's.'

'Who was the witness, Sheriff?' the deputy asked while his mouth was still full of food.

'It was Tom Brady from the livery. He saw an old guy coming out of the back of the saloon and running back into Main Street. Well it was more like limping according to Brady because the old guy had a gammy leg.'

Vogel nearly groaned once again when he heard the description that fitted Thomas perfectly. He'd heard all he needed to, and told Adley that he planned to head straight back to Statton Crossing before Thomas arrested someone.

'I think he forgets sometimes that he's hung up his badge, and can't go around arresting people. Hope to have that chinwag another time,' he added, trying to sound casual.

Adley looked disappointed. 'That's a pity because I don't get much chance to have an interesting conversation around here,' he replied. 'Most of the talk is about food.'

Adley's deputy was forcing a large chunk of bread into his mouth and the jibe was lost on him.

When Vogel headed out of Nashmora he kept his mount at a steady trot. There was no point in trying to catch up with Thomas, who would be well clear of the town by now.

Vogel could understand Thomas taking the money to make it look like a robbery, but it was hard to believe that he would kill a woman, killing a woman just wasn't Thomas, although there was no telling what he might have been capable of in his present mood.

Vogel was approaching the start of the hilly region a couple of miles out of Nashmora town when he heard the gunfire. The first shot was from a rifle, but the return fire was from a pistol. Vogel had learned the hard way that it didn't pay to get involved in trouble outside his jurisdiction, especially when it wasn't obvious who the innocent party was. The rocky terrain didn't give him the option to skirt around the trail so he proceeded with caution, hoping that the trouble ahead would have been resolved by the time he got nearer to where it had been.

A couple of minutes later he was beginning to think the incident was over, when the shooting started again; this time there was a heavy exchange of fire. At least he knew the identity of one of the antagonists when he saw

Thomas's stallion standing close by the rocks, clearly agitated by the shooting. Vogel pulled his mount up, but he had no idea what to do, especially as Thomas might be the guilty party. Perhaps someone had followed Thomas out of town, suspecting him of being the killer. But it was also possible that the man was Lee Molloy.

Vogel edged his mount closer to the spot where he suspected that Thomas might be taking cover.

'Marshal, it's Vogel,' he called out. 'Is that Lee Molloy up there, gunning for you because you killed Zak?'

There was a short delay before Thomas shouted back.

'It has to be, but I didn't kill Zak. Lee must have killed his brother over some trouble at the saloon.'

'You're the one with the motive, Marshal, and you were in Nashmora.'

'You can think what you like, but if whoever is up there with a rifle gets his way it won't matter none. He's already plugged me in the leg.'

Vogel didn't know what to believe, but he would side with Thomas for now.

'How bad is your leg, Marshal?' he called out.

'Bad enough, judging by the amount of blood I'm leaking.'

'I'll try and get to you, so hold your fire,' Vogel shouted back.

When Vogel made his move a bullet hit the dirt no more than six inches from his foot. He'd already taken his rifle from the leather scabbard strapped to his horse; now he fired off two rounds into the area where he believed the man was taking cover, then scurried to the next rock. Vogel started to work his way round towards his target, believing that the man had trapped himself in, confident that he would have the upper hand over Thomas.

'Marshal, I've got him pinned down,' Vogel shouted down towards the injured Thomas. When there was no response he shouted again, this time asking Thomas if he was all right, but the call was again met with silence.

Thomas had been drifting in and out of consciousness, weakened by the loss of blood. He had heard someone shouting, but he couldn't make out what was being said. He could see movement ahead of him, but he was having difficulty trying to focus on the blurred figure. Thomas heard the man curse after he slipped and fired in the direction of the sound. Thomas managed to fire off a second shot before he slumped forward and lost consciousness again.

Vogel reacted to the renewed shooting by sliding down the slope in his eagerness to reach Thomas, ignoring the danger that might still be present. Thomas was lying near a rock covered in blood, but at least he was alive. The fate of the man with a bullet hole in his forehead was in no doubt, but he couldn't tell if it was Lee Molloy because he'd never seen him close up before.

Vogel cursed when he discovered that his neckerchief wasn't long enough to use as a tourniquet to try and stop the flow of blood from Thomas's leg wound. He fumbled as he ripped the material in two and knotted the ends together. He managed to stop the blood and then led Thomas's horse close to where Thomas lay. He grunted as he lifted Thomas and placed him across the saddle, grateful that the horse had remained perfectly still during the operation.

He needed to get Thomas back to Nashmora as soon as possible, but he couldn't risk jarring Thomas too much and they would need to make regular stops to loosen the tourniquet. He had remembered Doc Jones telling him about the risks of losing a limb if a tourniquet was left tightened for too long. If Thomas survived, Vogel hoped he would still have the use of both legs.

★   ★   ★

As they entered Main Street, Vogel was hoping that the town had a medical man who could help the marshal. Not that he had much choice but to bring him here because it was doubtful if Thomas would have survived the extra distance back to Statton Crossing to be treated by Doc Jones.

Sheriff Adley was surprised to see Vogel again and shocked to see that he was covered in blood.

'Christ, Vogel, what's happened to you?'

'I'm fine, but Marshal Thomas is in a bad way and needs a doctor. He's outside.'

'Cyril, go and get Doc Healey and don't go via the diner, now move,' Adley snapped at his deputy. Vogel was surprised that someone with so much blubber could move as quickly as the deputy had just done.

Vogel and Sheriff Adley had just laid Thomas on a bed in one of the cells when Doc Healey came in with the breathless deputy behind him. Healey was no more than twenty-five years old and about the youngest medical man

Vogel had seen, but according to Adley they didn't come any better.

'Whoever applied this tourniquet might just have saved this man's life, and very likely his leg as well,' said Healey, his voice calm, then business-like as he ordered: 'I'll need some hot water and whiskey, and just one person in here to help me.'

Once again the deputy belied his weight and scurried off to bring the hot water from the diner which was at the far end of the street. When the deputy returned with the water and whiskey, Sheriff Adley left it to Vogel to assist the doctor by signalling to his deputy for them to withdraw from the cell.

Doc Healey managed to remove the bullet after a lot of careful probing. He dropped it into the metal bucket that contained an assortment of bloodied dressings. When he had eventually finished his work he turned to Vogel.

'I'm afraid I've done all I can for him. Now we need to give him plenty of fluids and hope that he's as tough as he looks.'

Vogel smiled.

'He's that all right. I don't know what he'll think when he wakes up in a cell. How long will it be before we can move him back to Statton Crossing?'

Doc Healey gave a huge sigh.

'I don't think we should be planning that far ahead. We'll need to take things slowly, but he'll live. The important thing is that he has someone with him for the next twenty-four hours, but he won't be going anywhere for about a week. He's had more than his share of lead, judging by the scars on his body, but I'm sure that he'll recover from this.'

★ ★ ★

Vogel had managed to snatch a brief period of sleep on the hard bed opposite the one where Thomas lay. He smiled at the thought that it must have been the first time that a sheriff and a former US marshal had spent the night in a cell. He'd been awake for a while, not wishing to disturb Thomas, when he sensed that he was being watched.

'Marshal, are you awake?' Vogel asked in a quiet voice.

'Who are you?' Thomas replied, his voice weak and croaky.

Vogel got up from the bed, dipped a cloth into the water jug, then invited Thomas to suck the liquid from the dripping material which he was holding against Thomas's lips.

'Who are you?' Thomas asked again when he had finished sucking the water from the cloth, 'and what have we done to be locked up?'

'I'm Sheriff Vogel from Statton Crossing, don't you remember what happened yesterday? You were shot while on your way home and I brought you back here.'

'So, how come we ended up in a cell and where's this place called Statton Crossing?'

Thomas had obviously lost his

memory, but otherwise he seemed fine, considering what he'd been through.

When Sheriff Adley arrived Thomas recognized him immediately, leaving Vogel puzzled by Thomas's failure to recognize him. Doc Healey called in later and explained that memory loss was a complicated subject and could be triggered by an emotional trauma. But after he had examined the back of Thomas's head and found severe bruising, which he concluded was the result of an old injury, he thought it was the more likely cause of the memory loss. Doc Healy fired a series of questions at Thomas which confirmed that there were strange gaps in his memory. He could remember his name, and where he was born. But he'd never heard of anyone by the name of Molloy and had no recollection of the incident in which he was shot, nor could he remember having a recent blow to the head. Vogel grimaced when the doctor asked Thomas if he was married.

'I was once, to my Mary, but she died

some years ago.'

The doctor applied a fresh dressing to Thomas's leg and then asked Vogel to help him prop up Thomas with a pillow and some blankets. When the deputy arrived with some food he was given the task of feeding Thomas, but he was soon sent packing with a growl.

'I'm not a baby.'

Doc Healey estimated that Thomas would need to stay where he was for a full week. There was a chance that the loss of memory might be due to a clot and that could prove fatal if he was moved too soon.

Vogel was tempted to ride back to Statton Crossing, but opted to check in at the hotel opposite so that he could be near Thomas if required. He was on his way to the hotel when he saw two men carrying a large bundle into the offices of Lincoln Snaith, the undertaker. It meant Vogel changing his plans and heading off to see Lincoln Snaith, who had been asked to recover the body of the man who had tried to kill Thomas.

Lincoln Snaith was a little man with a tiny black moustache. His face was pale and judging by the whiskey fumes that hit Vogel's nostrils when the undertaker greeted him, he was a heavy drinker. A point that was soon confirmed when he produced a bottle of whiskey and offered Vogel a drink.

Vogel declined the offer, but it didn't stop Snaith from taking a swig from the bottle before he spoke again.

'You've earned a drink, Sheriff, for the business you've brought me. That feller who was shot in the saloon and the lovely Melissa are in their boxes out there and they have just brought in the other feller. The men won't be having the fancy funeral that Madame Melissa will, but it's still good business and I thank you kindly.'

'Did you find his horse or any identification on the feller?' Vogel asked, ignoring the thanks that had been offered by the little creep.

'Melvin over there said there was no sign of a horse, nor was the dead man carrying any papers. Some no-good thief had even stolen his clothes. I was hoping you could give me his name for the records.'

Vogel explained that he had a good idea who it might be. There was also a chance that Marshal Thomas would be able to identify the corpse. But the body would have to be taken to the sheriff's office because the marshal couldn't leave his bed.

'That won't be a problem, but we'll need to tidy him up. He's just come in, and I haven't even had time to see him myself yet.'

Vogel hadn't got a proper look at the man in his haste to help Thomas and he asked Snaith if he could see the body.

'Of course you can. He's over there on the table. Melvin, let the sheriff see our new guest.'

Melvin grinned showing his yellow teeth.

'Is he a friend of yours?' he asked Vogel.

'Not exactly,' replied Vogel as Melvin

peeled the blanket away from the upper part of the body. 'Jesus, what's happened to his face?' Vogel asked when he saw the gory mess.

Snaith had joined Vogel near the table and looked down at the grotesque sight, appearing to admire it.

'If you or the injured marshal didn't do it then it was likely a mountain lion. I don't think even his own ma would recognize him now.'

When Vogel returned to the sheriff's office that night, ready to keep watch on Thomas, he heard him cursing and demanding to be let out. He calmed down when he saw Vogel, but still showed no sign that he recognized him.

Sheriff Adley gave the reason for Thomas's outburst.

'He wants to go and see who it was that tried to kill him before they bury the man tomorrow.'

Vogel explained to Thomas about the disfigured face of the man who was probably Lee Molloy. He had told the undertaker to bury him with Zak.

'The name means nothing to me. You'll have to tell me sometime why he was trying to kill me. I expect that I made a few enemies in my line of business.'

'So you remember being a marshal?' asked Vogel, encouraged by the reference to his past.

'Of course I do, but I wasn't just an ordinary marshal. I was a United States marshal,' Thomas said with pride.

The following day Doc Healey decided that Thomas no longer needed constant attention and Vogel headed home to Statton Crossing, promising to return in five days' time to pick up Thomas. He wasn't looking forward to the trip back because he would have to tell Adley that he believed that Thomas had killed Zak Molloy and probably Melissa as well.

★   ★   ★

'We thought you run off and got married, Sheriff,' was the greeting Vogel got from his deputy, Toby Jackson, when he arrived back in his office, followed by: 'Where the heck have you been?'

'It's a long story, Toby. I'll tell you about it later. How have things been here?'

'I think you might call it interesting,' replied Jackson. 'There's a surprise waiting for you in the cells. It's Molloy.'

Vogel didn't even wait to hang up his hat before he made his way to the cells. He was thinking that he'd made a wrong identification back in Nashmora, but it was Sheb and not Lee Molloy who was behind the bars.

'Old Sheb walked in here the day before yesterday and confessed to killing someone, but you'll never guess who. I told him to go home at first, thinking that he was drunk and perhaps wanted a break from his kids, but he insisted that he was telling the truth.'

Vogel was about to play a hunch and perhaps steal Jackson's thunder when he said:

'Sheb killed Zak in Nashmora as well as Melissa the saloon . . . 'Vogel paused as he was about to call Melissa a whore, but thought it disrespectful with her being dead, and simply called her 'girl'.

'Sheb didn't say anything about killing a woman. How did you know about Zak?' asked Jackson, when Vogel's comments had registered.

Vogel smiled as he tapped the end of his nose with his index finger to indicate that he had ways of knowing these things. He would let Jackson remain puzzled for a while before he told him about the events in Nashmora. He'd only guessed that Sheb had killed Zak because the witness's description of someone running away from the back of the saloon in Nashmora fitted Sheb just as much as it did Thomas.

Vogel spoke to Sheb later and learned that Zak and Lee had stolen money from a hiding-place at the homestead before he'd ordered them to leave. It was money that Sheb had saved to buy winter clothes for the children and that was why he went after them. Stealing from family was something that he couldn't abide. He'd gone to town first and discovered that the boys had headed for Nashmora. Sheb swore on his children's lives that he hadn't killed Melissa, nor had he stolen any money, and Vogel believed him.

When Vogel asked about Lee, Sheb told him that he had seen Lee leave the woman's room and ordered him to skeet. Lee wasn't a bad boy, just dumb for following Zak. Sheb's eyes had moistened when Vogel told him that Lee had tried to kill Marshal Thomas and now Lee was buried in Nashmora with his brother.

16

Thomas was sitting near Adley's desk when Vogel arrived to take him home to Statton Crossing. He was looking much better.

'Hello, Sheriff,' he greeted Vogel, but Vogel was visibly disappointed when Thomas added: 'I still don't know who you are, son.'

Thomas gave a broad smile.

'I'm only kidding, Vogel. I remember you now. According to Doc Healey you probably saved my life. I'm beholden to you for that and for coming back for me today. But if you tell anyone that I was locked up in a cell for a week then I'll whip your hide.'

Vogel returned the smile, relieved that at least Thomas was showing signs of improving.

Thomas had a surprise waiting when he got outside the sheriff's office.

'Now I do remember that feller, but how could anyone forget such an animal.' The stallion snorted and pawed the ground with one of its front hoofs when it saw Thomas.

While Thomas was busy patting the horse, Vogel managed to have a quiet word with Doc Healey. The doc advised against his telling Thomas the news about his wife, Olive. He suggested it would be better to wait and see how he settled when he got home before he risked shocking him with the news. Vogel sighed, still puzzled by Thomas's condition and the doc tried to explain once again.

'The fact is, Sheriff, we know very little about the brain, and there's no telling how things will improve. As you can see, there has been some improvement and we can only hope that it will continue. I'm sorry that I can't be any more helpful.'

As they were leaving, Vogel told Sheriff Adley about his conversation with Sheb Molloy and that he believed him when he denied killing Melissa or stealing any money. Adley said that he intended questioning Henry who had given up his job as barman. He'd been gambling heavily and buying expensive presents for one of the saloon girls.

*　*　*

During the journey back to Statton Crossing, Thomas had bouts of aggression as he tried to remember various landmarks. Some of them seemed familiar, but he couldn't put a name to them. He had calmed down by the time they reached Statton Crossing and Vogel reminded Thomas that he would have to trust him.

'I don't have any choice, son, because at the moment I feel like a stranger in my own town. I recognize that saloon there and the undertaker's, but not much more.'

'Howdy, Marshal, glad to have you back,' Merle Cawley called out as he swept the steps of his store.

'Howdy,' replied Thomas; then, after they passed the store, he asked Vogel who the man was.

When Vogel pulled his horse up outside his office, he suggested to Thomas that they should stop off there and have a drink before he took him home.

'It sounds like a good idea, son. Then, if you tell me where the cemetery is, I'd like to visit my wife's grave before I go home, wherever that is.'

Vogel was thinking about the doc's advice, but decided that he would have to do this his own way from now on. The young sheriff wasn't too keen on whiskey, but he poured himself a healthy measure after he had settled in the chair opposite Thomas.

Vogel cleared his throat and prepared himself before he spoke.

'There's something you ought to know, Marshal. It hasn't been easy holding things back from you, but it was thought best because of your memory problems. The fact is you remarried a while back to a fine lady, named Olive.'

Thomas could hardly believe what he'd just heard, not least because he felt it was a betrayal to the memory of his beloved Mary, but it must be true.

'Jesus, so I've got a little wife waiting for me at home and I don't even know what she looks like.'

Thomas repeatedly tapped the side of his head with his hand which was a habit he'd acquired since his memory-loss. It was an act of frustration, hoping that it would unscramble his memory.

'Olive, Olive, I know that name, but I'm sure she was married.'

'Her husband died,' commented Vogel, encouraged that Thomas at least had some recollection.

'I remember that now. Her husband was Henry; I forget his other name, but I remember that he died of the consummation, just like my Mary.'

His mind was in turmoil as he tried and tried to bring back his memory, but when he did, he wished he hadn't.

Thomas became agitated and shook his head from side to side, trying to remove the piece of memory that had just returned.

'But I can't see her, can I.' Thomas paused and then offered his own reason. 'Because my dear Olive is dead! I remember now, that's why I went to Nashmora after the Molloy brothers. She was alive when I left, but she died, didn't she, and I've got two graves to visit now.'

Vogel got up from his chair and went to comfort Thomas.

'Marshal, your wife is at home, waiting for you. She's fully recovered, but Doc Jones is still baffled as to how she did it.' Vogel took a hard swallow, smiled and then said: 'Welcome home, Marshal.'

'So it was the Molloys who attacked my Olive?' Thomas asked.

'That's a bit of puzzle, really, because despite what she told Doctor Jones about thinking there were two of them, your wife's not sure now. It seems that whoever it was attacked her from behind and she never got a proper look at them. We can never be absolutely sure it was the Molloys, but it seems very likely.'

Thomas knocked back the remains of the whiskey and stood up. He hadn't lost his sense of humour and reminded Vogel once more that he'd whip his hide if ever he mentioned that Thomas had spent a week in a cell.

Ten minutes later Thomas was knocking on his own front door, waiting to surprise his wife. When the door opened, he was beginning to think his memory was playing tricks on him, because the plump-faced woman standing in front of him wasn't the Olive he remembered.

Mrs Boscombe, who had been staying with Olive while she recovered, greeted Thomas and asked him to tell Olive that she'd gone home.

Thomas muttered his thanks to Mrs Boscombe and made his way into the house. It seemed strange to him when

Olive called out from the far side of the room:

'Ned, is that really you?' It was the first time that anyone had addressed him as Ned since his memory-loss. Thomas recognized the voice and the sweetnatured face of his wife who was smiling at him.

'It's me, honey, and I haven't forgotten what a lucky man I am.'

Thomas eventually released Olive from his embrace and asked her who the woman was who had answered the door to him. Olive thought he was teasing, but he wasn't.

17

Within a few weeks of returning home Thomas had recovered a lot more of his memory, but still couldn't recall the incident when he was shot by his unknown attacker on his way home from Nashmora. He had been remembering odd bits about his trip to Letana Creek and he couldn't rid his thoughts of the remarks that Doc Shultz had made about Mary Lowrie and Brannigan. He didn't know why it weighed heavily on his mind, but perhaps it would be clearer one day.

Thomas had been saddened when Sheb Molloy had been hanged, but he guessed the jury had no choice but to find him guilty.

He hadn't been too keen at first, but Olive had talked him into adopting two of the Molloy children, a boy and a girl. It meant that he would be able to teach the boy lots of things like pas do and he was thinking that perhaps, one day, a Molloy might even get to be a lawman.

★   ★   ★

Exactly five weeks after Thomas had returned home from Nashmora he received a letter which he had barely finished reading before he was reaching for his hat.

'I need to go and see young Vogel right away, honey,' he called out to Olive.

'But the pie's just about done and the potatoes are boiled,' she shouted after him.

'I'm sorry, Olive, this can't wait. I'll explain it all to you later.'

Thomas was like an excited boy bringing home the first fish that he'd ever caught when he burst into Vogel's office, and interrupted the conversation that Vogel was having with his deputy.

'I know who tried to kill me. The man buried with Zak Molloy isn't his brother, Lee, but there was a vague resemblance.'

'So who was it?' asked Vogel, eager to find out.

Thomas told him to be patient because he needed to tell him about his visit to Letana Creek first, now that he could remember it down to the finest detail.

It was quite some time before he finished.

'So now you know what happened when I went to Letana Creek,' he announced.

Vogel gave a short whistle.

'That's one hell of a complicated story, Marshal,' he said. 'So you think it was Sheriff Brannigan who avenged his brother and spun you a line about Lowry shooting you. There was something going on between him and the storekeeper's wife, wasn't there, and he's the one who came after you, isn't he, but why?'

Thomas smiled.

'I guess you'll have to improve your

detective work, son. But it was a former lawman who was trying to kill me when you turned up. It was Cliff Myers, the no-good deputy.'

Vogel shook his head and voiced his disagreement.

'He would hardly have ridden for three days just because you might have messed things up for him with his girl.'

'This letter is from Barbara Stone in Letana Creek,' said Thomas, holding it up. 'It was this that triggered my memory. I've been remembering bits and pieces about my visit to Letana Creek during the past week and this brought it all home to me. She told me that her daughter Shelley has been heart-broken because she hasn't seen Myers since shortly after I left Letana Creek. I'm not surprised, seeing as how he's buried in Nashmora. I knew the young feller would be hurting after what I did to him, but I never expected for him to come looking for me. He must have patched things up with Shelley before he came after me. I guess he must have felt more humiliated than I'd imagined.'

'It's a pity his face was messed up so much by the time I saw him in Nashmora, then you could have been absolutely certain,' said Vogel, still not convinced by what Thomas had said.

'There isn't any doubt in my mind that it was Myers. I can remember him coming down that slope just before I got my second shot off. I could see his busted nose and the blackness around his eyes as clear as I can see you now.'

Deputy Toby Jackson had sat listening to Thomas's story, fascinated by it. But now he had a sinking feeling in his stomach before he spoke.

'Jesus, Marshal, the feller that you described was here in this office.'

Thomas and Brannigan stared at Jackson, equally taken aback by what he had just said.

'When?' asked Thomas, beating Vogel to the question.

Jackson was now looking sheepish as well as awkward.

'It was while you had both gone to the Molloys,' he replied. 'It was the morning that your wife was attacked. I'm sorry, Marshal. I gave the son of a bitch directions to your house. He was wearing a deputy's badge and he said that he was an old friend from Letana Creek.'

Thomas turned cold at what Jackson's revelation probably meant. It must have been Myers who attacked Olive, not the Molloys. He might have ended up killing the Molloys for something they hadn't done if their pa hadn't got to them first.

'It ain't your fault, Jackson. Myers was a slippery eel and he told lies easily.'

It was Vogel's turn to remember something. He told Thomas that when he had visited Smith's undertakers after Myers's body had been brought in he noticed that Melvin, who had helped bring the body in, was wearing a deputy's badge. Melvin was a bit of a weirdo and Vogel didn't think anything of it at the time, but it looked as though Melvin might have stolen it from Myer's body to keep as a trophy.

* * *

Thomas wrote back to Barbara Stone and told her that he couldn't go into details, but she was to tell Shelley to try and forget about Myers because he wouldn't be returning to Letana Creek. Thomas was satisfied in his own mind about the killings at Letana Creek, but there were some who had their doubts!

After Jake and Matty had watched Thomas leave Letana Creek following the death of Lowrie, Jake had stroked his beard and was thoughtful before he spoke.

'I've been thinking about Lowrie being suspected for all them killings and for trying to finish off the old marshal. There's something fishy about it.'

It was Matty's turn to scratch his beard. His ears seemed to be having one of their good days, and he was hearing his friend quite clearly for a change. It might also have had something to do with the free bath that he'd had at Charlie's barber-shop yesterday.

'What do you mean, fishy?' Matty asked.

'Well, Lowrie never carried a gun. I remember him boasting once that he hadn't fired one since he was a young man and never planned to ever again. He reckoned it was uncivilized to carry a weapon. He might have said primitive, but I think he said uncivilized. You know what he was like for using them fancy words, but he was dead against firearms, I know that for sure.'

There was a long silence before Jake changed the subject.

'How long do you think the lovely Mary Lowrie will play the grieving widow before she lets Brannigan move into her bed?'

'Not too long,' Matty replied and grinned at the thought, 'Poor old Lowrie. Thought he was such a smart feller, but he never knew that while he was out at council meetings, Brannigan was likely giving his pretty young wife what she probably wasn't getting from him. Perhaps we should have told old one-eye about Brannigan and Lowrie's wife. I bet he would have been interested.'

Jake puffed on his old clay pipe.

'He'll be back one day to comfort Barbara Stone. They're a horny lot, these lawmen. But you don't know that Brannigan was up to anything with Mary Lowrie. We only saw them talking in the street just that once.'

Matty gave his friend a nudge.

'Yep, the old marshal looked the sort who would have an eye for the ladies,' he remarked.

Jake was doing his impression of a laughing hyena and Matty waited for the cackling to stop before he spoke.

'There's something else that might have interested the marshal. Remember he was asking about that feller Shacklade and we couldn't remember anything. Well, I can now. It came to me the other day.'

'You're not still thinking about Mary Shacklade,' Jake groaned. 'I've told you there never was a Mary Shacklade.'

'I ain't heard of a Mary Shacklade, but I knew a Mary Shackleton,' Matty replied, forgetting their previous conversation. 'Now I remember her. I wonder who she kept warm at night all these years. No, I was thinking of Robert Shacklade, or Bobby as he was known. I expect the marshal would be interested in what happened to him.'

Jake shook his head once again.

'He's the feller with all those flowers on his grave, but the marshal already knows about him.'

'But he don't know who killed him and why,' said Matty.

'I don't suppose anybody does now that they're all dead,' replied Jake. He stretched down to pick up the whiskey-bottle. There was a lull in the conversation before Matty calmly announced:

'I do.'

'You do what?' asked Jake after he'd poured them each a large glass of whiskey.

'It was Lowrie who shot that feller Shacklade and it was because he was sniffing after Evelyn Stone or Evelyn Lowrie as she became known.'

'You don't know that. How could you?' asked Jake, thinking that his friend was having one of his bad days in the mental department.

'Because I saw him do it,' replied Matty, still as calm as you like. 'I'd been laying traps up in the hills at Kriel's Eye and they were just below me. Josh Stone and Len Norris were there as well, but they tried to stop Jack Beamish and Lowrie beating up Shacklade. Shacklade managed to get free of them and he ran off while Josh was having a tussle with Lowrie. That's when Lowrie shot him in the back and not just once, but Beamish didn't even draw his pistol.'

'Well I'll be damned,' said Matty. 'You really did see it all. Mind you,

235

Evelyn Stone was a lovely-looking woman. Perhaps Josh kept quiet because of his sister. That might explain why Josh hated Lowrie's guts and never spoke to him after she died. Maybe Lowrie killed Josh and the others to keep them quiet.'

★　★　★

It was nearly six months before Thomas returned to Letana Creek with Olive to see Barbara and Shelley Stone, partly to have a break from looking after the Molloy children even though they loved them dearly. Lowrie's store had been taken over by Barbara Stone after Mary Lowrie left town, and Shelley was courting a nice young feller who helped out at the store.

The saddest sight for Thomas was the empty seats outside the saloon. He discovered that Jake had died just two months ago, and Matty had joined him in the cemetery a few weeks later.

Jake had died from natural causes, according to Doc Shultz. Matty had followed him because he'd lost the will to live. The night before Matty died he had trudged back to his tiny cabin, leaving behind an unopened bottle of whiskey beside the seat outside the saloon.

Before Thomas and Olive left Letana Creek he called in at the sheriff's office to enquire about Brannigan. He learned from the new sheriff, Tom Whittle, that Brannigan had left a few months ago. It seemed that Brannigan was upset about the rumours concerning him and Mary Lowrie, which he claimed were untrue. But the main reason was that he couldn't settle, feeling that he was to blame for the deaths. It didn't make him feel any better that he had probably killed the man who was actually responsible.

As Thomas reached the door of the office he turned and thanked the sheriff and expressed his disappointment that Brannigan had left.

'I hope he's still a lawman, wherever he is, because he'll make a good one with a bit more experience. I'm not one for gossip, but do you think there was any truth in these rumours about Brannigan and Mary Lowrie?' asked Thomas, unable to forget the lingering doubt that he had about Brannigan.

'I've heard those rumours as well, Marshal, but when Mary Lowrie left this town she was a very wealthy young woman and she was alone. When Brannigan left a few months later it was with one of the saloon-girls. So, my guess is that the rumours were false.'

Thomas was pleased with Whittle's answer, but followed it with another question.

'I wonder if he's still curious about who actually killed his brother? Of course, I'm forgetting you don't come from these parts and probably don't know what went on here, but it's too long a story to explain.'

'You mean Robert Shacklade?' said Sheriff Whittle. Before Thomas could recover from his surprise, Whittle added: 'Hang on a minute, I've got something that you might be interested in.'

Thomas was intrigued as he watched Whittle ferret through the heap of papers in the drawer of his desk. He handed over the faded envelope to Thomas.

'I found this when I was rummaging through some old documents in the little store room back there soon after I was made sheriff. It was a couple of weeks after Brannigan had moved on, but he had told me about his brother's death. He didn't seem upset by it. He said it was all a long time ago, but I guess he would have wanted to see that letter.'

Thomas opened the letter. It was addressed to Sheriff Todd Brewer. The writing was faded, but the anonymous message was clear enough. It read: *Jeff Lowrie shot Bobby Shacklade near Kriels' Eye.*

As far as Thomas was concerned the mystery was over. It was just as he'd told Brannigan while he was recovering in Doc Shultz's surgery. The interest in Robert Shacklade resulting from the appearance of the flowers must have spooked Lowrie. He couldn't run the risk of his name coming out when he was so close to his political ambition, so he killed all the men who might have revealed what he'd done. Thomas asked Whittle if he could take the letter so that it could be shown to Barbara Stone and the relatives of the other dead men and help dispel any rumours that their menfolk might have been involved in the killing of Robert Shacklade. The revelation in the letter would give them peace of mind and it would stop Thomas forever wondering about what the killings at Letana Creek had really been about.

We do hope that you have enjoyed reading this large print book.

Did you know that all of our titles are available for purchase?

We publish a wide range of high quality large print books including:
Romances, Mysteries, Classics
General Fiction
Non Fiction and Westerns

Special interest titles available in large print are:
The Little Oxford Dictionary
Music Book, Song Book
Hymn Book, Service Book

Also available from us courtesy of Oxford University Press:
Young Readers' Dictionary
(large print edition)
Young Readers' Thesaurus
(large print edition)

For further information or a free brochure, please contact us at:
Ulverscroft Large Print Books Ltd.,
The Green, Bradgate Road, Anstey,
Leicester, LE7 7FU, England.
Tel: (00 44) **0116 236 4325**
Fax: (00 44) **0116 234 0205**

Other titles in the
Linford Western Library:

THE HIGH COUNTRY YANKEE

Elliot Conway

Joel Garretson quit his job as Chief of Scouts to travel to Texas and claim his piece of land. He needed to forget the killings he had seen — and done — fighting the Sioux and the Crow in Montana . . . But he soon has to confront Texas *pistoleros* and then, aided by a bunch of ex-Missouri brush boys, he faces the task of rescuing two women held by *comancheros* in their stronghold . . . In the territory of the Llana Estacado, New Mexico, the violent blood-letting will commence . . .